SOMEWHERE

by the Sea

Finding SOMEWHERE Series
Book One

Verna Clay

The miserable have no other medicine but only hope.

—William Shakespeare

SOMEWHERE *by the Sea*
Finding SOMEWHERE Series
Book One

Copyright © 2016 by Verna Clay

VernaClay@VernaClay.com
Website: www.vernaclay.com/

Published by Verna Clay
Cover Design: Verna Clay
Picture: (© Karin Hildebrand Lau: Dreamstime.com)

Preface

I enjoy romance series that evolve gradually around small communities, and since Oregon is one of my favorite states, I naturally chose it for the location of my fictional town, *Somewhere.* To me, the name was perfect, because my desire was to create characters longing for acceptance and a sense of belonging "somewhere." And so, for the first book in this series, I introduce Faith Bennison, a woman who suffered the loss of two loved ones, and in the aftermath of tragedy, leaves her home in St. Louis to travel to the small seaside community of *Somewhere.*

I then fashioned a man who could restore Faith's happiness, Baxter Hope, but only after confronting his own demons.

And to add depth, mysteries were touched upon to be solved in future books. The main plot of each story, however, is resolved within that story.

And lest I forget, the heroes and heroines of *Somewhere* occasionally receive help from those residing on the "other side."

Verna Clay

Sequence of Books in the
Finding SOMEWHERE Series

Table of Contents

Prologue

As was her daily routine, Faith Bennison again opened the large tabletop picture book of Oregon's coastal towns and flipped to page ninety-two, the same page she studied every day. She knew every nuance in the photo—the way the sun reflected golden rays across the ocean at noon, the man fishing on the pier with his little boy beside him, and in the background a couple strolling hand-in-hand toward the end of the pier. Below that picture was another showing the curve of a beach with sunbathers along its shore and a close-up of five children playing in the water. She moved her gaze to the full page photo on page ninety-three showcasing a quaint and lovely town with outdoor cafes, antique shops, art gallery, beauty shop, clock shop, and in the distance, a large Victorian home. The caption below the picture said *Downtown Somewhere with Hope Bed & Breakfast in the distance.*

Releasing a long sigh, Faith returned to the previous page to stare at the man and child. The boy looked to be about eight, the same age her boy would have been had he survived the car accident that also killed his father. Faith traced her fingers over the paper people and swallowed the lump in her throat. For years, she and Hammond had dreamed about moving to a small town on the west coast, but his career, and life in general always got in the way. Now, three years after that terrible accident she was still perusing the same book that had given them such wonderful dreams. She closed her eyes and inhaled slowly, willing herself not to cry, but then suddenly she slammed the book shut and reached for her jacket. She grabbed her purse, pulled out her car keys, and rushed through the kitchen to the garage. Within minutes she was on the freeway and headed for the outskirts of town. At Horizon Cemetery she navigated a winding road and pulled to the curb, then, following a grassy

2

corridor bordered by graves, strode toward the ones she knew so well. Just as she reached the gravesites of her loved ones, an arrow of lightning streaked across the sky and buckets of water were unleashed. She ignored both and the earsplitting thunder that followed.

Kneeling between the graves she cried out, "I'm going to do it, Hammond and Charlie. I'm going to Somewhere." Another bolt split the sky and thunder rocked the ground. Prostrating her body between the graves in emotional pain, she sobbed, "I have to leave because if I don't, I'll soon be joining you."

1: Somewhere

WELCOME TO SOMEWHERE
by the Sea

Faith read the sign and couldn't believe she had actually arrived in the small coastal town of Somewhere. She drove past the sign onto Main Street, curious to see if the town resembled the photo she'd been studying for years. About a quarter of a mile from the sign she entered the town proper and inhaled sharply; it was even better than the photo. It was colorful and inviting, with vibrant flags decorating both sides of the street and the word "WELCOME" written in different languages on each one. Pedestrians strolled the sidewalks and entered brightly painted businesses of red, yellow, blue, green, and orange.

Faith was so caught up in what should have been a Norman Rockwell painting, that she didn't see the signal light turn green. A horn tooted behind her and she absentmindedly murmured apologies, even though the driver couldn't hear her. Slowly, she drove through town until she reached another light. After two more lights she came to a stop sign at the end of Main Street, which was intersected by a road that only turned south—Ocean Boulevard. On her right was the beautiful Victorian Bed and Breakfast from her picture book, but before checking in she decided to drive along Ocean Boulevard. She turned left at the stop sign to follow the shoreline and marveled at the azure sea mimicking the color of the sky. After passing a public beach and parking lot she reached a stretch of stunning homes on both sides of the boulevard, and then a marina. Tears stung her eyes as she said softly, "Hammond and Charlie, I'm here."

Gabby Evangeline Hope frowned at her son and replied to his remark, "Baxter, do you really think I don't know the plumbing needs updating?" She blew a wisp of hair off her forehead and smoothed her hands down her 1970s' style peasant blouse and tie-dye hippie skirt. At the age of fifty-seven she was several pounds overweight, but not concerned about it since she'd never been prone to vanity. She rarely wore makeup, or even visited Betty B. Breverton's Beauty Boutique. Her once brunette hair still reached her waist, but was now a lovely shade of silver. She supposed that by the time she was seventy, it would be pure white, and looked forward to that day.

Baxter said with exasperation, "Mom, why are you so stubborn? You know I have the funds to completely renovate this home." His voice rose in volume. "And if you don't do something soon you won't have a bed and breakfast."

Gabby's frown turned into a grin and she reached to cup her son's cheek. "It's not as bad as that, and you know it. You're a good man, Baxter, and I appreciate your concern, but you know I'd never take money from family members, especially my son. I've seen too many families torn apart by finances."

Baxter opened his mouth to counteract her, but Gabby continued, "Besides, I had a dream recently that things are about to change around here. I'm not sure if it's for the better or worse, but change is a comin'. However, if the plumbing fails, which it won't, I can always borrow money from the bank. Mr. Swift was telling me just yesterday that money is available if I need it."

Baxter puffed a breath. "Mom, the guy would *give* you the money. Why don't you just date him and put him out of his misery. He falls all over himself whenever you're around."

Gabby huffed, "Son, I can't believe you just said that. You know your father was the only man for me. He and I were polar opposites but never was a marriage more stable than ours. Why, we–"

"He's been dead for six years, Mom, and you deserve more than just this home–"

"I love this home! After your father inherited it from his father, he and I worked side-by-side to make it so successful. Why, people come from all over the country, and even the world, to spend time here and on our private beach, we–"

"You're talking to the choir, Mother. All I'm saying is having a man in your life might be exciting."

"And who are you to talk? Where's the woman in your life? Where's the excitement?"

Baxter lifted his hands in surrender. "Point taken. But at least I date occasionally."

Gabby lifted her shoulders and stood as tall as her 5'5" frame allowed. "This conversation is over. Your room is ready for you and the account books are on the desk in the sitting room." She glared at her son. "You're staying the entire summer, aren't you?"

Suddenly, Baxter grinned and hugged

his mother. "I always do. Besides, you know how much I love trying to untangle your accounting."

Gabby chuckled and returned his hug. "You realize, don't you, that we have a verbal sparring match every summer."

Baxter stepped back and held his mother's shoulders. "Looks like this one will be no different. It's going to be a long, argumentative one, Mom."

Gabby grinned. "I'm looking forward to it."

2: Owen

On her return trip along Ocean Boulevard Faith pulled into the public beach parking lot and parked her Toyota Camry in a space next to a family of four unloading beach paraphernalia from a van. Two boys, the oldest who looked to be around nine and the youngest six or seven, were squirting each other with water pistols, and their mother stopped what she was doing to chastise them. "Robbie and Lonnie, if I have to warn you one more time, you'll both be grounded from swimming for an hour!" She glanced at Faith who was exiting her car. "Boys!"

Faith gave her a fake smile and nodded. She needed to get away from this family. If she didn't, she might burst into tears. Stashing her purse in the trunk, she grabbed a water bottle and towel and hastened to the beach. Walking past the pier she had viewed so many times in her tabletop picture book, she couldn't believe she was actually here. Three fishermen were scattered across the pier and a man walking his dog reached to pet him.

Being a weekday the beach wasn't overly crowded and Faith followed the shoreline. She spotted a boulder that lent shade from the sun and spread out her towel. She then discarded her T-shirt in favor of the tank top beneath and rolled the cuffs of her shorts higher. Leaning back on her elbows she watched waves ebb and flow. The beach was perfect for children and the family she had parked beside was now walking past her. The young mother waved at Faith and smiled, as if they were friends. The father, carrying an umbrella and beach chairs, laughed with his boys and even started to awkwardly chase them, hampered by his cumbersome load.

For a moment Faith visualized herself as the mother and Hammond as the father walking the beach with Charlie. She closed her eyes and listened to the family's laughter, pretending all was right with her world. Seconds later she opened her eyes and stared blankly at nothing. All was not right. Her husband and son were dead and she was sitting on a beach in Oregon two thousand miles from the home they had lived in, and wondering what to do with the rest of her life. Her house in St. Louis was on the market because living there day in and day out with the imagined voices of her loved ones, was making her crazy. Every time a floor creaked or a shutter banged, she turned, expecting to see her husband or child—expecting they could somehow feel her misery and would appear one last time to say goodbye. The very fact that she'd been unable to say goodbye compounded her sadness exponentially. She closed her eyes again seeking peace in the sound of the waves, and unexpectedly felt something nudge her foot.

She jerked her eyes open. A large red dog, probably a collie mix, was pushing a Frisbee against her toe as he retrieved it.

For a moment she forgot her sadness and reached to pet the dog that had paused to watch her. "Hello there. Aren't you a handsome fellow?" She gazed around for the owner and saw a boy of maybe nine or ten wearing a blue ball cap approaching her. Her heart twisted.

"Hello, ma'am. I'm sorry about my dog bothering you."

Faith swallowed against the lump in her throat. "He didn't bother me."

The dog returned to the boy who was only a few feet away and laid the Frisbee at his feet.

Against her better judgment, Faith said, "What's your name? My name is Faith."

The boy picked up the Frisbee and said, "Owen." He tossed the toy down the beach and the dog ran after it.

"Do you live in Somewhere?" she asked.

"Yes."

He didn't say anything else so Faith volunteered, "I just arrived today. I'll be staying at the Hope Bed & Breakfast for a while."

The boy's face lit up. "Miz Gabby is a really nice lady and she bakes the best cookies. You'll like her."

Faith's mouth lifted in a smile. "Oatmeal raisin cookies are my favorite. I hope she bakes them."

"Oh, she does. She makes all kinds of cookies. She even sells them at Mr. Lucky's Grocery. The store is only two blocks from Miz Gabby's house and I work there part time. Mr. Lucky pays me to help him stock shelves after school." The boy stopped speaking when his dog returned with the Frisbee and again dropped it at his feet. Owen bent to retrieve it and said, "Guess I better go. But I'll see you again and maybe we can help each other." He turned and ran down the beach.

Faith didn't understand his parting words, but watched him for a long time before lying back on her towel and covering her eyes with her forearm. It was a struggle to keep from crying.

An hour later she strolled along the shoreline enjoying the feel of wet sand beneath her feet. When the sun was past its zenith her stomach growled and she started walking back to the boulder to retrieve her towel. She needed to check in at the bed and breakfast which would begin a new phase of her life, but for some reason she was reluctant to do so. Would doing so distance her from Hammond and Charlie? Would their memories begin to fade? She didn't want them to fade.

She passed a volleyball game in progress and the participants were the family with two boys. The mother whacked the ball, lost her footing, and tumbled laughing onto the sand. She smiled up at Faith. "Hello again."

Faith returned her greeting and added, "You have a beautiful family."

The woman opened her mouth to reply, but Faith was already rushing away. She didn't want to be drawn into a conversation about anyone's family.

3: Gabby

Returning to the intersection of Main Street and Ocean Boulevard, where Hope Bed & Breakfast was the last business on Main Street, Faith followed the driveway of the B & B to a parking lot at the back of the Victorian manor. For long moments she sat in her car and gripped the steering wheel. Her lengthy, cross-country journey was about to end and she wondered if her emotional journey would also end, or at least get better. She had all summer to find out. After making the decision to come to Somewhere she had called the B & B and worked out arrangements for a long-term stay, and although expensive, it was much less than the nightly rate. And even if she hadn't gotten a break on the cost she would have stayed for a few weeks anyway, before finding a less expensive place. Her husband's life insurance policy had been more than adequate and now it was time to fund her new life.

The back door of the home opened and Faith watched a tall man, probably about her age, mid thirties, with short-cropped black hair, carry a bag of trash to a green painted enclosure that blended with the surrounding foliage. On his way back to the house he paused when he saw her, nodded, and then continued to the door. Faith wondered if he was the custodian or maintenance man, and then discarded that notion. There was something commanding about his presence, as if he were a man of some stature in the community. Perhaps he was the owner of the B & B. Soon she would find out. Garnering her courage she reached for her purse and decided to retrieve her suitcase later, just in case her escape from her former life was a mistake and she needed to hightail it back to St. Louis. In her heart she knew that wouldn't happen, but just knowing she could run was comforting.

She stepped from her car and followed a pink, azalea bordered pathway that led to the main entrance. She paused when she reached the porch steps and the wheelchair ramp beside it. Inhaling a calming breath she whispered, "Hammond, I'm here. Let's see if this home is everything we dreamed of." She climbed the steps and again paused at the screen door. The inside door was open and she could make out a foyer. Beside the entrance was a sign that read:

WELCOME TO
HOPE BED & BREAKFAST
A HAVEN FROM THE STORM

Faith's eyes got stuck on the word "HOPE" and started to sting. Immediately, she entered the B & B to keep her emotions from overpowering her yet again, and stopped short. She turned in a circle studying the lavender walls, moss green panels, and sunflower yellow molding of the foyer.

"The colors are unexpected, don't you think? I always get the same reaction from people who haven't been here before."

Faith turned to face a woman who had obviously been part of the hippie movement. She was smiling widely and stuck out her hand. "Hello, my name is Gabby Hope and I'm the proprietress of this monstrosity. Are you Faith Bennison?"

"Yes. How did you know?" She shook Gabby's hand.

My son, Baxter, was just taking some trash out and saw your car. He noted the license plate was from Missouri, and since you registered with an address in that state, I took a wild guess."

Faith shifted the strap of her purse to her other shoulder and found herself smiling at the engaging woman.

Gabby said, "Follow me and we'll get you signed in. Then I'll show you to the pioneer bedroom that you requested. If you change your mind, however, the Queen Elizabeth room is available."

Faith followed Gabby to what had

probably been a parlor, but was now the check in station, with its elegant freestanding counter strewn with a collection of brochures and business cards in ornate holders. Everything from sunset cruises to jet skiing, trail hikes, and fishing were advertised. The remainder of the room was furnished with a redwood antique writing desk with a Queen Anne chair, and three French Gentlemen's chairs. The walls of this room were painted yellow with lavender panels and green molding. The Gentlemen's chairs were purple and the affect was literally breathtaking.

"What do you think about the colors in here, Faith? They're the same as the other room, but coordinated differently."

Faith accepted the pen the proprietress handed her and said before completing the information form, "They're exquisite. You certainly have a talent for dramatic color combinations." A minute later she handed the form and pen back to her hostess.

"No, hon, you keep the pen. As for my color choices, some guests take one look and cringe, which doesn't bother me. A long time ago I learned that I can't please everyone or fit into their mold, so I don't even try." She slipped the paper into a drawer and pushed a guestbook toward Faith. "One more thing, please sign our guestbook." After Faith signed the register that had entries from all over the United States, Gabby continued, "So, Faith, I remember speaking with you on the phone when you made your reservation, but I didn't get a chance to ask what brings you to Somewhere?"

Glancing away from Gabby's intense blue gaze, Faith replied honestly, "I decided to change my routine."

There was a short silence before the hostess replied, "Well, hon, Somewhere is the best place in the world for changing routines. We got tons of extracurricular activities, but the best part about our town is that it isn't on the mainstream radar because most folks are drawn to

22

Brookings south of us. So if its solitude you want, there's plenty of that, too." She motioned toward the door. "But we can chitchat later. Let's get you settled."

They reentered the hallway that ran the length of the house to stairs at the back and paused at the entrance to a formal dining room on their left. Gabby said, "This is where all meals are served, unless, of course, you want to eat in your room or on the second floor balcony. We have six bedrooms for guests and there's a brochure in your room giving mealtimes and other particulars. We try to be as accommodating as possible, so let us know if you have a favorite food or there's anything you need to avoid." She pointed to a closed door at the back of the dining room. "The kitchen is through there. We modernized it about five years ago and you're welcome to join our cooks at any time. They love mingling with guests. They're a young couple that I hired out of Dallas about two years ago. We also have a fulltime housekeeper and two part-time workers who fill in wherever their needed." She continued toward the stairway still talking nonstop.

At the top of the stairs the landing faced a stained glass window of yellow sunflowers and then continued along the eastern and western sides of the house, so that from anywhere above, the main floor was visible below. Ornate railings as high as Faith's waist kept the landing safe, and on both sides were four doors.

Gabby said, "My son and I live on the third floor, which is reached from a stairway at the back of the kitchen. Years ago, when my husband was alive, we remodeled the old servants' quarters into a sitting room, two bedrooms, and added a bathroom. Baxter lives in California, but spends his summers with me." She pointed to the center door on the western landing. "That's the pioneer room and it has its own bathroom, as you requested. The Queen Elizabeth room which is directly opposite does too. The other guests share a bathroom." She pointed to the first doors on both sides of the landing. "Those are the bathrooms." She paused for breath and pulled a key from her pocket as she walked to the western side. "All the bedrooms have doors that open onto balconies that run the length of the house. The eastern rooms have a view of town and the western, the ocean." She handed Faith the key. "You go ahead and open the door since it's your room."

4: Baxter

Baxter glanced up from the computer screen in the sitting room on the third floor and grinned at his mother. "Did you get the new guest settled in?"

"I did and she's a strange one. She carries sadness around her like a cloak. I'll bet my bottom dollar something terrible happened to her."

Baxter grunted. "Well it's a good thing I'm handling your bottom dollar then."

Gabby smiled at her only child. "You're just like your father. He always said we'd end up in the poor house if I was in charge of our finances." She sighed. "And he was right. I'm a sucker for every salesperson and charity event."

"And that's why you have me." He hesitated and added, "So, if this gal…what's her name…"

"Faith Bennison."

"…suddenly hits you up for money, you better call me. I don't trust sad, head cases."

"You're just jaded because your wife was a sad, head case who fleeced you in the divorce."

"You got that right. So I'm more discerning about people than you are."

"I don't agree." She laughed. "See, there we go again, disagreeing, and you've only been here two days."

Baxter tried to suppress a grin as he returned his attention to the accounting program on his computer.

After calling her only family member to let her know she had arrived in Somewhere, Faith said goodbye to her sister Melody and sat on the rustic log bed to peruse her surroundings again. With every go-around, she saw something new and interesting. She'd already noted that the frame and headboard of her bed were hand-hewn pine logs and the pretty yellow and blue wedding ring quilt was hand-stitched. She fluffed one of the plump yellow pillows and lay back. Her gaze circled the room and rested momentarily on each furniture piece: a natural finished pine dresser with two matching nightstands; a rocker formed of twisted Manzanita branches with a seat cushion matching the blue of the quilt; a maple secretary desk; and a small, drop-leaf oak table with two chairs. The room was a mish-mash of different woods, but the affect was eclectic and enchanting. On the whitewashed walls were a couple of black and white photos of ocean scenes and also framed magazines dating as far back as 1901. On the wall across from the bed was a flat screen TV. In addition to a door opening onto the balcony, there was one window with pretty white lace curtains.

Rising from the bed Faith stuck her head in the bathroom again to admire the claw foot tub and fluffy blue towels embroidered with one word, "HOPE." Although small, the bathroom was quite adequate. She walked to the balcony door and stepped outside into a cool breeze that ruffled her hair. On the B &

B's private beach she watched waves lap the sand. A handful of sunbathers lay on towels and a mother sat with her child building a sand castle, or rather a blob they piled higher and higher. She walked to the railing and moved her gaze away from the private beach to scan the shoreline all the way to the other end of the cove, where the marina was barely visible. The headland at that end was similar to this end with its forested peninsula, and covering the distance between the peninsulas was the public beach and expensive homes along Ocean Boulevard. She returned her gaze to the private beach that gave way to scattered boulders and then the evergreens and wondered if there were trails leading into the forest. She would ask Gabby.

As she was about to turn away, she caught sight of the boy and dog she had met earlier. They were now at the edge of the private beach, right before the boulders, and the child was still tossing the Frisbee for his dog. While the dog chased the toy, the boy looked in her direction and waved.

During dinner Baxter studied the profile of their latest guest when she turned her head to converse with another guest, and decided his mother was right. She did wear sadness like a cloak, and if he hadn't been older and wiser than he'd been at the age of twenty-five when he'd met his future wife, he'd be tempted to feel sorry for her. It was her eyes that gave her away. They were the color of dark chocolate, large, with long lashes, and profoundly sad. Her eyes were beautiful.

Realizing his mother was asking him a question he quickly turned his attention to her and saw her self-satisfied expression. She'd wanted him to become interested in another woman for years, and now she'd caught him studying Faith Bennison. He answered her query and then politely continued conversing with their guests. Currently there were eleven guests—three sisters, a young couple with a toddler, an elderly couple, a middle-aged couple, and Faith. The dining table could accommodate twenty people, but rarely did they have more than sixteen.

One of the sisters, probably in her late twenties, began flirting with him and asking questions about the area. She invited him to join her and her sisters that evening for a bonfire on the beach and he politely declined with an excuse that sounded reasonable. He had no inclination to become involved with any woman, much less a bed and breakfast guest. Back in California there were a couple of women he dated and occasionally bedded, but they were no more interested in a long-term relationship than he. Faith was asking his mother a question and he reined in his thoughts to listen to her.

"I was wondering if your peninsula is open for exploration. If so, are there hiking trails? I would love to walk through the trees."

"Yes, the land is open to our guests. My husband Marcus inherited the peninsula and this home and we remodeled it into a bed and breakfast thirty years ago. He died a few years back and I've maintained two of the trails he loved. If you follow the main trail, which runs west, it intersects another heading north. The northern trail takes you to another harbor on the other side of this one and the western trail ends at the apex of the peninsula, where the founder of the town, Oliver Hope, built what's been dubbed Stone House." Gabby grinned at her guests. "The house was built around 1890 and abandoned in 1910 when this home and two identical ones were built. The new homes were for the senior Mr. Hope and his twin boys who were about to marry. Mr. Hope's home burned down in the 1960s and the other one was turned into a museum that's on Second Street. There are signs in town pointing the way." Her grin widened. "And as for Stone House, there are rumors that it's haunted."

The sisters gasped.

Gabby turned to Faith. "Would you like Baxter to accompany you on a walk?"

Baxter almost choked on the water he was drinking.

Hastily, Faith said with a stricken look, "No, no. I don't want to trouble anyone."

Her response made Baxter feel so bad that he tried to sound convincing when he said, "It wouldn't be any trouble at all. I'd love to show you around."

Faith met his gaze and said flatly, "No. I really don't need a guide."

Candace, the sister who had been flirting with him, smiled seductively. "I'd love to see a haunted house with you as my guide."

Turning his gaze on Candace he glimpsed his mother's amusement. "It would be my pleasure to act as guide for you ladies." He made sure his comment included all the sisters. He didn't want any alone time with Candace.

5: Trail

The next morning after a delicious breakfast of waffles and pure Vermont maple syrup, scrambled eggs, home fried chunks of potatoes, and strawberry tarts, Faith decided to explore the wooded area of the cove. Wearing a fanny pack with her water bottle and cell phone in it, she headed across the beach for the boulders and then the forest beyond, searching for the trailhead. Being a small woman, barely five feet, she had always envied tall, robust women that could hike for miles, run marathons, lift heavy weights, and jog alongside their husbands. Faith's husband had been athletic and competitive, often competing in bike and running marathons. Once, when she had expressed her frustration about her small stature, he'd laughed and pulled her into his arms, kissing her passionately and whispering in her ear, "You're perfect just the way you are." He'd nipped her earlobe and added, "And sexy as hell."

He'd then easily lifted her and carried her to their bedroom.

Faith paused at the tree line and swiped away the tear trickling down her cheek. Refusing to entertain additional memories, she continued her search for the trailhead. She'd walked probably less than three hundred feet when she spotted it. Surrounded on both sides by ferns, the trail dipped slightly as it ventured into the darkness of thick foliage. She stepped onto the path and abruptly stopped. For some reason her heart was pounding. She placed her palm over her chest and said softly, "You're just reacting to Gabby's theatrics about a haunted house." Her reasoning slowed her heartbeat and she continued into the coolness of the forest. Within a few steps she was surrounded by such dense greenery that the outside world was no longer visible. She shivered and walked deeper into the unknown on a mission of discovery. After maybe ten minutes she came to the intersecting trail Gabby had mentioned and sat on a fallen log. She closed her eyes, inhaled the scent of damp leaves from bigleaf maple trees and the needles of Douglas-firs, western hemlock, Sitka spruce, and other conifers, and listened to the cry of gulls. Finally, she stood and made a decision to follow the northern trail to the other cove.

Her imagination soared as she skirted ferns, gazed upward at moss dripping from tree branches and particles of dust sparkling in the sunlight. She listened to a cacophony of birds and envisioned pirates hiding stolen gold in deep holes or hidden caverns and their treasure-laden ships being ruled by a one-eyed, patch-wearing captain who governed his lackeys with an iron fist. Before the death of her husband and son she had even entertained the idea of writing adventure stories, but that dream had died with them.

The walk turned out to be longer than expected and she stopped several times to snap photos with her cell phone.

Occasionally, the sun broke through the tops of the trees and stippled the ground in golden light, which made for beautiful pictures. She stopped walking when she spotted bright sunlight glinting off water. The golden light was beautiful and beckoned her forward.

Suddenly, a figure stepped into the light and Faith squealed. The man had his back to her, but jerked around. It was Gabby's son, Baxter, and for an instant he seemed blinded as he stared into the shadows of the trees. Then he said, "Hello, Faith. I'm sorry I startled you." He stepped forward and it was as if her pirate had come to life. Her voice wouldn't work and she must have looked dumbfounded, because he said, "Are you all right?"

She had to physically and mentally glance away from the tall man to recover her senses. Returning her gaze to his, she said, "Ah, yes, I'm fine. I guess I wasn't expecting to meet up with anyone, which is silly because I'm sure many people walk these trails." She was rambling and shut her mouth.

Baxter now stood in front of her. "Not as many as you would expect." He chuckled. "Maybe it's because of the haunting rumor. Anyway, I love the view from this side of the cove. Come on and I'll show you."

Faith followed Baxter into the sunlight, where, indeed, the view was stunning. He explained, "Hope Cove circles around to this cove that's a flora and fauna refuge maintained by the forestry service, so no one is allowed in." He motioned to a nearby boulder. "Have a seat."

Faith accepted his invitation and watched waves lap the narrow beach below the bluff they were on. It was about a hundred feet to the bottom with no avenue that she could see for climbing down. The beach encompassed the cove and beyond it were craggy boulders. Beyond the boulders was the forest.

Baxter had also taken a perch on a fallen log. "Most of the year I live in San

Jose, so spending summers here helping my mother with the bed and breakfast is a treat. I enjoy starting my day by jogging here or to Stone House."

Faith felt Baxter staring at her as she continued watching the waves.

He said, "I figured you'd start exploring today, but I expected you to go to Stone House first. That's what most serious hikers do when they find out how old it is."

Smiling, she glanced at him. "I was saving the best for last, but maybe this is the best." She waved her hand outward, encompassing the cove.

Baxter returned her smile. "Both have their selling points."

They continued to enjoy the view and make small talk for several minutes. After a short silence, Baxter said, "I guess I better head back and get to work. Would you like to come with me or stay here?"

"I think I'll stay here and watch the waves." After he left she began composing a pirate tale because she knew the identity of the captain.

6: Jennie and James

Faith returned to the B & B and spent the rest of the day in her room, not because she didn't want to explore the town, but because she had an overwhelming desire to write. The story took on a life of its own as she began creating an historical romance about a swashbuckling pirate named Dax. Of course, she never expected it to be read by anyone, so Baxter would never know he was her model for Dax. She even grinned at her audacity.

She tapped the story into her laptop until three and didn't even think about eating until her stomach growled. Hoping to find a bowl of fruit downstairs, she saved her file with the title of Dax, and then brushed her straight, auburn, shoulder-length hair. She applied some lipstick before going in search of something to tide her over until dinner. In the dining room she was relieved to find bowls of apples, oranges, bananas, and peaches on the sideboard and grabbed a banana.

"Oh, there you are," said Gabby. "We missed you at lunch and figured you were either exploring the town or the cove. Did you eat lunch?"

Faith grinned sheepishly. "Actually, no. I was in my room working on something and overlooked the time. Did missing lunch cause you a problem?"

Gabby made a tsking sound and glanced at the banana in Faith's hand. She motioned toward the kitchen door. "No problem, but let's go find you something more substantial than a banana. Besides, I want you to meet our chefs, Jennie and James Pierson, affectionately known to everyone as J & J who work at the B & B. She grinned at her silliness and Faith returned her grin. For Faith, Hope Bed & Breakfast was turning into a wonderful place to regroup.

Gabby continued, "You didn't meet J & J sooner because they took some much needed R & R to spend with their kids.

Goodness, soon I'll be talking in shorthand." She pushed the door open and Faith entered a large, country kitchen with pots hanging above a massive island. The cupboards were open-concept and displayed vast amounts of plates, bowls, cups, saucers, and serving dishes. A huge window brought light and beauty into the room with a view of the B & B's private beach and forested peninsula. She had entered a cook's heaven.

Immediately, Faith recognized the couple she had avoided the previous day at the beach. Jennie glanced up from the food processor she was operating, turned it off, and grinned at Faith. James placed a tray of cookies onto a cooling rack and also grinned. Gabby made introductions while he removed his oven mitts.

Jennie said with a western accent, "It's a pleasure meetin' you, Faith. I saw you at the beach yesterday and was gonna invite you to join us in a game of volleyball, but you seemed to be in a hurry. Maybe we'll get a chance to play volleyball before you leave."

Before Faith could respond, James said in the same accent, "Nice meetin' ya, ma'am."

Faith smiled at the couple, knowing she would never join them on the beach. The heartache of watching them with their children would have been too much. She said, "It's a pleasure meeting you, too, Jennie and James."

There was an awkward silence and then Gabby said, "Faith missed lunch. Is there any chicken pot pie left?"

Faith started to protest, but Jennie gushed, "Yes, ma'am. It'll only take a sec to warm up."

The growling of Faith's stomach kept her from further protest.

After Jennie warmed the pot pie in a microwave, set it on a tray, and added tableware and the iced tea Faith had asked for, Gabby invited her onto the front porch to eat.

Faith wanted to return to her room to

enjoy her meal and reread what she had written, but decided it would be rude after Gabby's kindness. She joined her hostess on the porch that ran the width of the house and faced Main Street. Remembering the question she'd been meaning to ask, she said, "How did Somewhere get its name?"

Gabby chuckled. "It was really the perfect name for the town because the founder, Oliver Hope, after making a fortune with an import business, sold his San Francisco based operation to pursue a simpler lifestyle. He uprooted his wife and twin sons to travel the coastline looking for that perfect life and ended up in Oregon. It's reported that his wife, growing weary of travel said, 'You better find somewhere soon,' and shortly thereafter they entered this cove. Her husband then told her, 'Looks like we've found Somewhere.'"

"What a great story," said Faith, using her fork to break into the flaky, golden crust of her pie. Lifting a morsel of

46

chicken she blew on it and gingerly placed it in her mouth. It was still hot, but deliciously so. She closed her eyes and moaned. "This is awesome."

Gabby laughed. "I've gained fifteen pounds since J & J started working here."

Faith enjoyed another bite as Gabby motioned toward the boulevard. "Some of the homes on the boulevard are owned by part-timers who like to spend summers here, and I have to tell you, the houses are incredible. Can you imagine owning a four or five thousand square foot home that you only visit for a few weeks each year? And many are larger than that."

Faith shook her head. "Not really. And besides that, this town is so picturesque I'd want to make it my permanent home." She closed her eyes again as she enjoyed a forkful of creamy vegetables.

When she opened them, Gabby was grinning widely. "J & J are the best cooks in town and I'm blessed to have them. They relocated to Somewhere about five years ago from Dallas, where they worked for some high class restaurant. They said they were sick of the big city and wanted to raise their children in a community where locals weren't strangers on the street. When they first arrived they stayed here and when I found out they were chefs, I invited them to give my B & B a shot. They did, and the rest is history."

Faith picked up her spoon so she could include the juice of the pot pie in her next bite.

Gabby continued, "They've got a home near the top of Hope Hill behind us that, in my estimation, is a better place to live than the boulevard because of the elevated view. Seeing the entire cove from above and the endless blue beyond is incredible. And storms during fall and winter are indescribable sights when the sky and ocean turn gray, and you can't decide where one begins and the other ends." She got a faraway look as if reliving the scene, and suddenly Faith

wanted to experience one of those storms.

When Gabby returned her attention to Faith she smiled sadly. "My husband died of a heart attack during a storm and you'd think I'd hate them, but I don't. Somehow they make me feel like Marcus is standing beside me." She chuckled. "Maybe it sounds crazy, but storms make me feel good, and the worse they are, the better." She reached to pat Faith's shoulder. "Perhaps I'm speaking out of turn, but there's sadness in you. If you ever need to talk about anything, I'm here."

Faith cleared her throat, said abruptly, "I'm a widow, too," and changed the subject. "I haven't explored downtown yet. I think I'll go there tomorrow. Is there any place I shouldn't miss?"

Calmly, Gabby responded, "Be sure to visit the museum." Then she named other places of interest. Faith finished her meal, stood to leave, and thanked Gabby again for her hospitality. As she was about to enter the house Gabby said softly, "Find your storm, Faith."

7: Sandy

All night Faith dreamed of raging storms and woke several times to the silence of a serene summer night.

Find your storm...find your storm...find your storm. Was there anything in this world that could help her heal? Help her continue a life void of her family? Bring her peace?

Waking to the depression she fought daily and that had kept her bedridden for weeks after the accident, she forced herself to rise and shower. She was going to explore town, come hell or high water.

During breakfast she learned that the elderly B & B guests had checked out and two brothers now occupied their room. The brothers were young, maybe late twenties, handsome with scruffy, unshaven jaws, and kept glancing toward the three sisters. Faith suppressed a smile. Three brothers, instead of two, would have been perfect; however, since

Candace directed all of her attention at Baxter, maybe two brothers worked well for the situation. She glanced at him to see him watching her. She feigned indifference even though her heart jumped, which was distressing, because she had no interest in pursuing a relationship with a man; be it friendship or anything else.

Gabby said to the group as a whole, "What do you think of these pecan pancakes? Jennie's trying out a new recipe, so we're all guinea pigs."

There were immediate responses saying how delicious they were and Faith joined the praise after swallowing a mouthful of the melt-in-your-mouth, crunchy pecan cakes dripping with maple syrup. The conversation, as it often did, then revolved around food, and Faith thought about the boysenberry pancakes she used to make for her family. She almost mentioned them, but stopped herself in time. In no way did she want to be questioned about her family.

Like Gabby, maybe everyone could see her sadness, but there wasn't any allegorical "storm" that could restore her happiness. She finished her pancakes, took a last sip of coffee, and excused herself.

Directly across from the B & B was a small park at the apex of Main Street and Ocean Boulevard, and she made a mental note to visit the park and walk the boulevard on another day. She walked east on Main Street toward the shopping and tourist district and the first shop she encountered was a lovely boutique called Bathing Suits Galore. There was a salesclerk in the display window dressing mannequins in hot pink bikinis and Faith paused beside a second window of mannequins dressed in black, one-piece suits. She was impressed with one that had yellow piping around the bodice, and when she envisioned her old brown suit, she cringed. The thought of wearing that outdated monstrosity propelled her into the boutique. The clerk, still in the window, lifted her head to smile and welcome her with a joke. "Good morning! Just give me a minute to get this mannequin decent."

"Take your time. I'll just browse." Faith found the rack of black bathing suits and searched for size five or six. She found a size five and removed it from the rack.

The clerk stepped out of the display window and although she wasn't pretty in the classical sense, she had the kind of face not easily forgotten. Beneath wildly curly muddy blond hair that was tamed by two large clips on the sides, her almond shaped green eyes, long nose, overly large mouth, and pointed chin, were stunning in combination. Her most amazing feature, however, was her golden tan, and although slightly overweight, she wore the extra pounds well in turquoise slacks and a matching shell. The yellow scarf tied around her shoulders and gold dangling earrings added contrast. Her makeup was flawless and not excessive. Instinctively,

Faith knew that if she ever wanted a makeover, this was the woman to seek advice from. The clerk said, "My name is Sandy and I love that bathing suit because it's understated, yet striking with the yellow piping. The dressing room is in the back if you want to try it on."

Faith studied the suit for a second. "Yes. I think I will." Five minutes later, preening in front of a mirror she whispered to herself, "Faith, you are going to buy this suit and sunbathe. You may even venture into the ocean." Giving her body a once over, she decided she was too thin. Maybe J & J's cooking would add the ten pounds she needed. She heard the clerk outside the dressing room asking, "Do you need another size?"

"No. This one is perfect. Thank you."

After dressing, she returned to the front of the store where the clerk was rearranging scarves on a display rack. The friendly woman glanced up and smiled warmly. "Are you visiting

Somewhere? If so I can direct you to several local attractions."

Faith liked the clerk's attitude. "Sandy, I'm Faith. And yes, I'm visiting. I'm staying at Hope B & B."

"Nice to meet you. Be sure and tell Gabby and Baxter that I said hello." She glanced at the bathing suit. "Would you like me to ring it up?"

"Yes." Faith lifted a lovely blue and beige scarf from the display that mimicked the colors of sea and sand and handed it to Sandy. "And this scarf, too."

While Sandy rang up Faith's purchase, she said, "I've lived in Somewhere since I was twelve. My mom and dad decided this was the perfect place to raise their only child, so we moved here from Seattle fifteen years ago." She paused in sharing her history to tell Faith how much she owed and began bagging her purchase in a pretty white bag. "Sometimes I show up at the B & B for lunch, so maybe we'll see each other again." She accepted the cash Faith handed her.

"That would be nice," Faith responded and then asked, "If I were looking to purchase a home here, who would you recommend as a realtor?"

Sandy handed Faith's change to her. "Oh, that's easy; Dave and Doris McGovern. They're some of the friendliest people you'll ever meet and they know every inch of Somewhere. They're completely honest and above-board about every house they show. In fact, they sold me one four years ago that's three blocks behind my shop. I really wanted a view, but those houses were more than I could afford, so the McGoverns found one that I could easily build a deck on the roof. I followed their advice, hired a local contractor, and now I have a million dollar view on blue collar wages."

Faith accepted her purchase, thanked Sandy, and turned to leave, but before she reached the door Sandy called out, "Wait! I think I have a business card for the McGoverns in my purse." She excused herself, entered the back of the store, and returned a minute later holding up a card.

Faith thanked her and asked, "Is there a great place nearby to eat?"

Sandy enthusiastically suggested Mama Pink's Diner. "If you stay on Main Street, it's at the halfway point of downtown. You can't miss the hot pink exterior."

Faith said she would definitely try out the diner and then bid Sandy goodbye. As she continued down the road she found herself doing something she hadn't done for a long time—spontaneously smiling.

8: Mama Pink's Diner

Inhaling deeply, Faith enjoyed the fresh, salty air as she continued her exploration of downtown Somewhere. The main shopping district consisted of several blocks and was resplendent with colorful facades and business signs with such interesting names as: Mama Pink's Diner, Betty B. Breverton's Beauty Boutique, Handy Dan's Hardware, and Classy Coffee Cafe. It was obvious that the city planners did not require coordination of colors, such as in other cities, and the overall affect was quaint and eclectic because each business was unique unto itself.

Faith paused in front of Mama Pink's Diner and perused the posted menu of DOWN HOME COOKIN'. A chalkboard beside the door advertised the daily special.

TODAY'S SPECIAL - $9.95

Best meatloaf and mashed potatoes you ever tasted, with homemade sourdough bread and your choice of veggies! And our famous marionberry pie!

Continuing down the street Faith decided she would try some of that marionberry pie on her way back to the B & B. She walked three more blocks, visited a couple of antique shops and a clock shop, and then crossed the street to enter Art's Art Gallery. The artworks included paintings in several mediums, glasswork and pottery, wood carvings, and bronze and clay sculptures. The wood carvings of sea animals mounted on driftwood were intricately detailed and very expensive.

A thin, short-statured man approached Faith after she had perused the gallery for a few minutes. "Welcome to my gallery. I'm Art Hope. Please let me know if there's anything in particular you're looking for."

Faith was surprised by his last name.

"Are you related to Gabby Hope?"

The gentleman smiled. "Yes. Her husband and I were distant cousins. Are you staying at the B & B?"

"I am, and I'm very impressed."

"Gabby is a genius when it comes to hospitality. Welcome to Somewhere."

"Thank you. This is my first foray into town and I must say it's one of the loveliest I've ever visited."

"I couldn't agree more."

Faith motioned to the carving of a starfish. "These wood carvings are astounding. Is the artist local?"

"Yes, but he doesn't want his identity known." Art chuckled. "He signs each one with 'Beach Bum' and is becoming nationally popular."

"He's very talented."

The proprietor then began pressing Faith about her art preferences and suggesting several pieces. Finally, she said, "I'm just browsing for now."

With a resigned expression Art inclined his head across the room. "I'll be at my desk if you need help."

Faith continued strolling through the gallery until she thought she'd seen everything. She was just about to leave when she spotted an alcove she had missed. Entering it, her eyes widened when she felt something akin to static electricity lift the hair on her arms. There were six paintings of scenes depicting various aspects of daily life in Somewhere, but the artist had cleverly intermingled two timelines on the same canvas: a modern day one and another from around the turn-of-the-century. However, there was one painting that was different. It was a boy and his dog playing on the beach. The boy was wearing a blue ball cap and had tossed a Frisbee into the air that the dog was chasing. Faith thought about Owen and his pet, and stepped from the alcove to ask the owner if the picture was of them, but he wasn't at his desk. She returned to study the painting once more and searched for the artist's signature. It was signed simply, "Vee." The other pictures were also signed in the same manner. Since Faith didn't want to wait for Art to return from the back room or have him pressure her into buying something, she left the gallery and started walking back in the direction of the B & B.

When she was across the street from Mama Pink's Diner, she jaywalked to the other side. She entered the diner and realized every table was taken; even the counter at the back was packed. A sign just inside the door read, "Welcome and Seat Yourself!"

Faith was about to leave when a waitress wearing a pink T-shirt and carrying a tray loaded with three plates of meatloaf and mashed potatoes, called from across the room, "Honey, your best bet right now is to sit at the counter until a table opens up. There's an empty stool on the end."

Faith glanced at the counter again and saw the stool. Smiling at the middle-aged woman with ponytailed bleached blond hair sprouting brown roots, she nodded a response because answering would have required her to shout. As soon as she sat at the counter a glass of water was placed in front of her by an elderly woman also with a ponytail and wearing a pink T-shirt. She looked to be in her seventies with massive fine wrinkles—not the deep etched kind—covering every inch of her face and neck. She was tall and big boned and her hair was shockingly pink. Her bone structure was such that it was obvious she had once been a stunning woman. She grinned at Faith. "Howdy. My name is Edna Jolene Elizabeth Pink, otherwise known as Mama. Are you staying in Somewhere or just passing through?" Although her greeting was direct and somewhat abrasive, Faith took no offense and instinctively knew that Mama Pink was a wonderful woman.

A sudden clatter interrupted the buzz of conversation and Faith turned to see a young woman, probably not more than twenty, bending over a tray of drinks and ice scattered across the floor. The poor girl with a brunette ponytail and wispy bangs looked like she was about to cry and Mama called out. "Now Suzy, honey, don't you worry about that. If I had a dollar for every tray I dropped, I'd be a rich woman."

Faith watched the first waitress and another one rush to help the young one. Even some of the customers jumped from their seats to assist as a busboy hurried to the scene with a broom, dustpan, and mop. Quickly, the disaster was cleared and everything returned to normal.

Mama Pink, who had stepped from behind the counter to speak with the mortified waitress, gave her a quick hug and returned to Faith. She pointed to a vacant table. "We got an open table now if you want it."

Faith shook her head. "I think I'll stay here."

Mama said, "And what can I get for

you? Today's special is our most popular."

"Maybe next time. Right now, I'd like to try that marionberry pie with a cup of coffee."

"You got it."

For thirty minutes Faith enjoyed her pie, chatted occasionally with Mama, and found out the woman's last name was really Pink.

Mama refilled Faith's coffee cup and said, "I think the stars must have been aligned just right when I was born. My favorite color has always been pink and this diner was a success from the first day it opened back in the '60s. And I let every man I married know that I was keeping my maiden name. Some of 'em squawked about it, but I stood my ground and refused to marry 'em until they agreed."

Faith wondered how many times Mama had been married, but refused to ask something so personal.

Mama continued, "My first husband

even had the nickname of Pinkie. My second husband, Roberto, showed up for our first date in a pink Cadillac. And just to let you know, everything they say about Latin lovers..." she winked, "...is true. And I could go on and on about my five husbands, but I'll save that for another time."

During the course of their intermittent conversations Faith learned that Harriet was the bleached blond waitress, and Julie, the second waitress—a younger version of Harriet—was her daughter. And, of course, Suzy was the sweet girl who had spilled the drinks. Faith mentioned that she was staying at Hope B & B for the summer and Mama said, "Gabby and me go way back. We get together at the B & B sometimes and gossip." She grinned. "Join us and you'll learn some of Somewhere's secrets."

Faith laughed. "I may just do that." She ate the last of her pie, finished her coffee, and decided that Mama had an endless supply of talking points, and if she didn't break away, she'd be there the rest of the day. Mama bid her a cheerful goodbye and made her promise to return.

Faith jaywalked again to the other side of the street and spent an hour exploring. She came to a sign with the word MUSEUM and an arrow pointing down a side street and walked in that direction.

9: Hope Museum

The museum was on Second Street and Faith was feeling excited about learning more of the history of Somewhere. She'd heard tidbits at the B & B and Mama Pink's Diner that piqued her curiosity, and she wanted to fit the pieces together, especially if this was where she chose to relocate. Hope Museum was two blocks off Main Street in a Victorian mansion that, except for paint color, was identical to the B & B with three stories, balconies on both sides of the second floor, and a veranda spanning the front of the house. A white wicker settee and four matching chairs blended beautifully with the pristine white veranda and balconies. The body of the house was painted pale blue with beige shutters, no doubt chosen to mimic sea and sand. Faith loved the affect and hastened up the porch steps. Next to the door in a white wicker basket were multiple brochures advertising local attractions, restaurants, and guided tours. An OPEN sign hung next to the door and below the sign was another one indicating the museum's hours and entrance fee of five dollars.

As soon as Faith stepped inside the home she recognized the same layout as the B & B. A woman dressed in a green period costume dating to the Victorian era stepped into the foyer and enthusiastically greeted her.

"Welcome to Hope Museum! My name is Vicky Patterson. Please take your time and enjoy your visit, and just so you know, this house is one of three built by the Hope family in 1910. Oliver Hope, the founder of our town, and his twin sons Sebastian and Randall, each had a home."

Faith immediately liked Vicky and commented on her attire.

Vicky smoothed a hand down her skirt. "This is one of my favorite dresses and I actually sewed it myself. I created a pattern after I saw the dress in a 1910

Sears and Roebuck catalog."

"Wow! I can't imagine sewing something so intricate. How long did it take?"

"It took about a month, but it was a labor of love because I love the Victorian era."

Faith confided, "I'm actually staying at Hope Bed & Breakfast and I find the history of Somewhere fascinating. I understand the three houses are identical."

Vicky looked delighted when she responded, "Yes. However, Marcus and Gabby Hope remodeled the second floor of Sebastian's home years ago to add two bedrooms and extra bathrooms to their B & B. They also remodeled the third floor for their living quarters." She made a waving motion. "This home belonged to Randall Hope and Oliver's home was built atop Hope Hill. Sadly, the house burned down decades ago and now there's a lookout where it used to be." She paused for breath and smiled.

"What can you tell me about Sebastian and Randall?"

"Now that's an interesting story. It's said that the brothers were very close until they had a falling out over the fate of Somewhere back in the 1920s. Randall wanted to build a hotel and turn the area into a tourist destination and Sebastian wanted it to remain pristine and natural. Eventually, their father was so angry at his sons' public feud that he took action. He divided the cove into three sections. The southern end he gave to Randall and the northern to Sebastian. The central portion he placed in a trust to be governed by the town's elected council members. Needless to say, Sebastian wasn't happy about that and feared that one day a greedy council would cave to the interests of outsiders. To some townspeople that happened when a portion of the land was rezoned and sold for housing along Ocean Boulevard during a financial crisis in the 1980s, but so far, big business hasn't made any inroads into Somewhere. Our town remains a peaceful haven for tourists and residents."

Faith said, "Ocean Boulevard must have brought in a substantial amount of money. The homes are very expensive."

Leaning close, Vicky said, "Let's just put it this way. The last house sold for over four million." She grinned. "The locals call it Millionaires' Row. However, you have to remember the original plots were sold over thirty years ago and home prices have skyrocketed since then. Are you looking to buy?"

Faith chuckled. "If I was, I couldn't afford anything there, but I think I'd rather live on Hope Hill for its view. Do you live in town?"

"Actually I live on the third floor of the museum. Leo Constanzo, the owner of this home, is a wonderful man, and because I'm supporting my mother, he offered me this job and living quarters several years ago." Explaining further, she said, "Mr. Constanzo is the widower of Loretta Hope, the granddaughter of Randall."

"So he's related to Gabby Hope by marriage?"

"Yes. She owns the northern cove and he owns the southern. Both sides of the cove passed into their hands after their spouses' deaths."

"What an interesting family. Maybe I'll meet him at the B & B."

Vicky's expression became serious. "Actually, remember that split between the families? Well, Gabby and Leo don't much get along. I guess the grudge between the twins is still alive and well among them."

That revelation surprised Faith because Gabby didn't seem the type to carry a grudge, much less one as old as that. But rather than ask additional questions because it would appear nosey and rude, she turned her attention to her surroundings. "Where do you suggest I start my tour?"

"Many guests, especially the women,

begin in the kitchen. I'd take you on a tour myself, but my helper is out with a cold so I need to stay in the foyer."

"Not a problem, and beginning in the kitchen is a good idea."

Vicky walked to the desk beside the door and picked up a brochure. "This brochure gives excellent descriptions of the rooms and some of the history of the home and town. And if you have questions, I'll do my best to answer them."

"Thank you." Faith accepted the brochure, paid her five dollars, and followed the main hallway to the dining room. Passing through that room she entered the kitchen through the connecting door. The kitchen wasn't modern in any sense of the word and she felt like she'd just stepped back into the early 1900s. A large and sturdy table dominated the center of the room, with freestanding storage shelves against the walls. Faith was amused by the kitchen gadgets displayed on the table and shelves: jelly molds, apple corer, orange squeezer, egg coddlers, flat iron, pie crimper, rolling pin, odd shaped culinary utensils, and multiple other curiosities. A massive cook stove dominated one wall and displayed a copper tea kettle, iron skillet, and waffle iron. Another storage shelf was packed with plates, bowls, and serving dishes.

After viewing the kitchen, Faith returned to the dining room with its faded floral wallpaper of red climbing roses amidst swirling green vines. In the center of the room was a round oak dining table with a sturdy central support having claw feet that matched the claw feet of the six chairs. The table was covered with a faded lace tablecloth and set with beautiful, raspberry red chintz floral china. Along one wall was a matching oak cabinet displaying additional china from the same set and on the opposite wall was the buffet.

Next she entered the library that was equally as dated and charming, and finally the parlor, which had been turned into a souvenir shop. After that she headed upstairs. The first bedroom she explored was formal and bland, just the opposite of her comfortable and homey one at the B & B. The room had two wooden chairs with tall backs, one of which was placed before an open rolltop desk with an ink well and quill pen next to faded paper. The bed was a simple four poster with no engravings and no canopy, and the bedspread was a quilt sewn of monotone shades of brown squares. Heavy brown velvet draperies had been pulled aside to allow a shaft of light in, but still the room was dim. The only color came from a lavender pitcher and matching basin on a tall table near the window. The freestanding wardrobe, open to reveal period clothing, was engraved with a couple of flourishes, but just as bland as everything else in the room. Faith stepped closer to inspect the clothing items. Two faded dresses, a beige one and a brown one, looked cumbersome and uncomfortable. A drawer in the wardrobe had been pulled out to reveal a faded corset and other undergarments. Faith shook her head, thankful that she hadn't been born in that time period.

The other bedrooms in the house proved to be more cheerful and colorful and the baby's room, next to the bland one, was particularly delightful with a canopied bassinet, baby buggy that had obviously been restored, rag dolls, and sepia pictures of a chubby little girl from birth to around age three. In one of the photos the grinning child appeared to be about two years old and was wearing the same outfit that was preserved under glass and hanging on the wall. Her pretty ringlets showcased an adorable smile. Below the photo was a metal placard that read, ROSE MERIDITH HOPE. Faith decided to read the brochure Vicky had given her for more information about this intriguing family and gasped at what she discovered. She would ask Vicky to expound on it.

For over an hour she wandered the house and mused over its furniture and innumerable interesting objects. When she returned to the foyer Vicky was sitting behind the small greeting desk reading a book. Throughout Faith's investigation of the home a few tourists had arrived and she'd passed them in the hallways or entered rooms they were already in, but for now, the entrance remained empty. Vicky glanced up, laid her book aside, and said, "What do you think? Is this an era you would have wanted to live in?"

Faith shook her head. "Not at all. At least not after I saw those cumbersome dresses and corset. How about you?"

Vicky's smile was sadly sweet. "Actually, my name is Victoria and maybe there's something to that, because I would have loved living in the Victorian age." Her countenance brightened. "The room with the corset belonged to Belinda Hope, wife of Randall. Their daughter,

Rose, mysteriously disappeared at the age of three and Belinda never recovered. By all accounts, the once cheerful, gregarious woman remained in perpetual mourning and gave away all her beautiful clothing. It's said that she wore the dullest of dresses until at the age of forty-one, she also mysteriously disappeared."

Faith said, "I was shocked when I read about their disappearances and that they were never found."

"Yes. It's quite the mystery. After the courts declared Belinda dead, Randall remarried in his late fifties and had two children, a son and daughter. His daughter was the mother of Loretta Hope who married Leo Constanzo, the man I told you about who owns this home and the southern cove, also the marina. As for the mystery, everyone in town, past and present, has their own version of what happened to the first wife and child. Most folks speculate there was foul play—murder or kidnapping—although a motive has never been explained. The family was rich, yes, but as far as is known, ransom notes were never received. As for murder, it hasn't been established why anyone would want to murder a beautiful child or her mother years later, or even if the disappearances are related." She blew a breath. "Makes no sense. Of course, since the husband is always a suspect, Randall was investigated, but never charged with anything."

The sound of footsteps on the porch interrupted the history lesson and Faith said, "Wow! What a strange family history."

Vicky nodded, "I know."

The front door opened and several tourists entered. Faith said quickly, "Thank you for your hospitality. And now that I'm fascinated by this home and its history, I'll be back."

Vicky grinned. "Please tell Gabby I said hello."

After leaving the museum Faith was

feeling both physically and emotionally exhausted. The thought of someone's child simply disappearing was unthinkable. At least in Faith's situation, she knew what had happened. She couldn't imagine living year after year not knowing, and her heart went out to the parents, Randall and Belinda Hope.

Baxter stood at the window in the sitting room of the third floor and watched Faith Bennison turn into the walkway of the B & B. From that height he had a sweeping view of Ocean Boulevard, the public beach, the southern cove with its marina, and the vast blue ocean. He returned his attention to Faith as she approached the porch steps. She intrigued him, which his mother had obviously surmised since she'd made sure to let him know Faith was a widow. He wondered if their guest's sadness had anything to do with the loss of her husband, and suspected it did.

He moved away from the window

when he lost sight of her at the porch steps and returned to his desk to continue the task of making sense of his mother's crazy accounting. For being such a savvy businesswoman, her bookkeeping skills drove him crazy, and when he'd asked for an explanation as to why a thousand dollars was given to the "Let's Revive Woodstock Foundation," she'd merely looked at him like she couldn't believe he was asking such a dumb question and said, "I can't believe you're asking such a dumb question. Woodstock's message was love and peace, something this country desperately needs."

Baxter shook his head and grinned. He wouldn't trade his mother for the best soccer mom in the history of motherhood, and he wondered if Faith had children.

10: Stone House

Over the next week Faith explored much of Somewhere, and the more she saw, the more she fell in love with the town and its residents. They were quirky, kind, funny, and intriguing. She returned to Mama Pink's Diner for the meatloaf special and enjoyed every bite. She even felt like she'd gained a few pounds since arriving, which was a good thing.

A few days after her visit to the museum, she returned and continued discussions with Vicky about the early settlers of town, and when her new friend invited her to coffee on Saturday, she readily accepted.

Now, sitting in a small room that had once belonged to a servant, but was furnished as a tiny sitting room and fitted with a sink, hotplate, and microwave, Vicky poured jasmine tea from an ornate teapot into dainty teacups painted with Monarch butterflies and said, "As you can see, I love everything Victorian." She handed the lovely teacup and saucer to Faith and then invited her to enjoy the bonbons, nuts, cookies, and sweet breads set before them. The women faced a small window with only the sky visible to them and Vicky continued, "I've remodeled this top floor in my mind many times, replacing the window with a large one, but, of course, that will never happen. I would refuse such a change because it would damage the originality of the house. The only concession I made when I moved in was for Leo to create this tiny kitchen and a bathroom.

Faith said, "With this being a museum, I can understand your reasoning, but if it weren't, would you remodel it like Gabby has? I haven't seen the third floor, but I imagine it's quite nice."

Vicky sipped her tea and smiled. "Yes, her remodel is lovely. They knocked out walls to create a large sitting room, added a bathroom, and updated the two remaining servants' bedrooms for themselves. But to answer your question,

I guess I'm a throwback to another age. Even if this weren't a museum, I wouldn't remodel." She looked sheepish. "Sometimes I even pretend I'm living in the era of this home. And when things go bump in the night, they don't scare me. I figure it's just a previous occupant experiencing a moment of nostalgia."

Faith's eyes widened. "Are there many bumps in the night?"

Vicky laughed. "No, not many, but if you want a place with more than that, you should go to Stone House out on the northern peninsula."

"You mean the first house built by the town's founder?"

"Yes." She leaned forward. "It's locked up, but ever so often tourists or locals who explore the grounds tell of strange happenings."

Faith also leaned forward. "Like what?"

Vicky said softly, "They tell stories of voices coming from inside the home and a dog's bark outside, but no dog around. There have even been reports of male and female apparitions in Victorian dress."

Vicky's cell phone rang and the women jumped. Vicky laughed and glanced at the caller ID. "It's Mr. Constanzo." She answered, "Hi, Leo," and smiled at Faith. She listened and said, "That's great. I'll be right down with my new friend, Faith Bennison, who's staying at Gabby's place." She paused and listened again. "Okay. See you in a second." She hung up. "The owner of the museum is downstairs. He wants to see my idea for a new brochure. Come on. He's really nice."

Faith followed Vicky downstairs to the foyer and saw a tall man reading entries in the guestbook. He glanced up when he heard them and smiled warmly. He was probably in his late fifties or early sixties and still a very handsome man: tall with a touch of gray at his temples blending into thick black hair, a lithe but solid body evidencing a healthy lifestyle, and a friendly smile with beautifully straight white teeth. Faith wondered if he wore dentures, but quickly cast that notion aside when she stepped close enough to shake his outstretched hand after Vicky made introductions.

Leo Constanzo said, "It's a pleasure making your acquaintance, Ms. Bennison. I hope you're enjoying your stay in Somewhere."

"Thank you, Mr. Constanzo, but please call me Faith. And yes, I love everything about Somewhere."

"And you must call me Leo. I'm addressed as Mr. Constanzo every day at work and frankly, after hours, I ask everyone to call me by my first name."

Vicky had walked to her small desk and removed a piece of paper that she now handed to her employer. As she began explaining her drawing for a brochure, Faith noted that she was an excellent artist. Leo added a few ideas and they quickly decided to go with the new look. He then engaged Faith and Vicky in a short conversation about a storm expected to arrive within a day or two. After he left, Faith returned with Vicky to her sitting room, where they warmed their tea in the microwave and spoke about the town's annual outdoor market. Vicky said, "Main Street will be closed at both ends and filled with vendors. We get lots of artists, photographers, health food sellers, farmers, jewelry makers, birdhouse builders, junk food peddlers, and more. I'm going to have a booth representing the museum and that's why we redesigned the brochure."

Vicky's cell phone rang again and she frowned. "Excuse me. This is my mom."

Faith glanced at her watch. "No problem. I need to leave anyway. I'll pop into the museum next week to say hi. Don't worry about showing me out."

Vicky nodded and answered her phone. "Hi, Mom. Are you feeling better?"

The next day after breakfast Faith stepped onto the balcony and scanned the sky. In the distance low lying gray clouds contrasted with blue skies directly overhead. Leo had said a storm was approaching, so Faith vacillated between staying in her room and writing her pirate story or taking a walk in the woods. The walk won.

The foyer and dining room were empty and she considered going to the kitchen to let someone know where she was headed, but since she had her cell phone, she decided it wasn't necessary.

After her first excursion into the forest she had returned only once and still hadn't gone as far as Stone House. Now, with the sun shining and clouds far in the distance, the day was perfect for an adventure to the headland of Gabby's peninsula.

She walked past the private beach and a few sunbathers to reach the scattered boulders, and then the trailhead. When she came to the fork, she reconsidered going to Stone House because if she veered north, she would once again find herself at the lovely overlook of the adjoining cove, but then she might run into Baxter. Although she saw him almost every day, she always felt tongue-tied around him. He was very attractive and carried a commanding persona that intimidated her.

She continued westward with the sun dappling the ground through breaks in the trees, but the air suddenly cooled and the sky darkened. The storm clouds that had been so far away were now overhead. For a moment she considered running back to the B & B, but a fat raindrop made it through the tree branches and landed on her cheek. She was closer to Stone House than the B & B, so she rushed forward. She figured she could take cover under an eave at Stone House.

The sky blackened even more and a bolt of lightening temporarily illuminated the trees before thunder shook the ground like an earthquake. It was then that Faith wished she had told someone where she was going. They probably would have talked her out of it. She reached into her pocket to retrieve her cell phone and check the signal strength. There were no bands.

By now, torrents of water were breaking through wind slashed trees and soaking her. She started running as fast as feasible toward the house at the end of the trail.

Another lightening bolt streaked through the sky, closer. She ran faster. When a third flash lit the air, she stopped and placed a hand over her heart. In front of her on a bluff was Stone House and beyond it, the raging sea.

11: Rex

Running to Stone House, Faith reached the backside and cowered under the overhang. From what she had seen during the lightening flash it was one story and not overly large, and to weather such storms for over a hundred years, it had to have been solidly built. Slowly, she edged from the back of the house to the southern side which seemed more protected from the wind. She continued along the wall, passed a window that was securely boarded from the inside, and paused at the front corner.

Another flash brightened the sky and gave her a momentary glimpse of the front of the house which faced the sea. Again, she was amazed at how solid the house remained after so many years. She was standing at the edge of a low stone porch that, except for rotted railing, appeared intact. Rather than step onto the porch through a gap in the disintegrated wood, she returned to the shelter afforded by the southern wall. When there was a break in the storm she slipped through the gap and rushed to the front door. As she had expected it was locked. The storm raged anew and another flash revealed that the railing on the northern side was new. Obviously, someone was restoring the porch, but that didn't help her now. She noted a window beside the door that was also boarded. The wind's ferocity picked up and lightening flashed multiple times in succession.

Faith hurried back to the shelter on the southern side and huddled there. Over the next hour she shivered with cold, but stayed crouched in the best location available. And while she shivered she berated herself for her naivety of coastal squalls. She would never make that mistake again.

The air darkened even more and that's when she began to actually fear for her safety. Was she in the midst of a hurricane? The storm grew louder and surprisingly she thought she heard the voice of a child calling out, "Rex!" Was it only the wind? Was it her imagination?

She jumped to her feet and ran from the shelter of the building toward the edge of the bluff looking for a child. She squinted into the dim light and waited for the lightening to flash again. When it did she saw nothing other than an empty bluff and waves raging beyond the promontory. Rain pelted her face. She turned to search the land behind her and screamed as a dark shape rushed forward.

Faith started to run but then struggled against powerful arms holding her prisoner. She kicked, yelled, and fought with strength garnered from an adrenaline rush before she honed in on a voice. "Faith, stop it! It's Baxter! I'm trying to help you!"

Baxter? Her assailant was Baxter? She stopped struggling and allowed him to draw her to the safety of the porch. He stepped away from her. "I've got a blanket in my backpack for you."

Faith felt weak with relief knowing that she'd been found and sagged against the stones of the house. She closed her eyes and a moment later felt a blanket being spread over her shoulders. She reached to pull it tightly around her and opened her eyes to see Baxter squatting low enough so that he could look directly into her face. His concern made her wince.

"What are you doing out in the storm? And why were you on the bluff in such weather? If one of the guests hadn't seen you headed toward the forest and become concerned when you didn't return, you might have been stuck outside for hours."

Faith replied weakly, "Thank you." Baxter leaned closer and she said louder, "Thank you! I had no idea the weather could become this terrible in such a short time." Then she remembered the child's voice. "I thought I heard a child calling for someone named Rex. That's why I was on the bluff. I was looking for the child.

Did you hear anything? Do you think we should search?"

Baxter suddenly straightened and Faith glanced up. His expression had morphed from concern to what looked like anger.

She repeated, "Did you hear anyone?"

"No. There's no one."

Lightening flashed and Faith jumped. As thunder rocked the ground, Baxter clasped her arm and called above the storm, "We need to get inside the house." He pulled her toward the front door and reached into his rain slicker pocket for a key. After a couple of twists of the doorknob it opened.

12: Warmth

Faith entered Stone House and Baxter picked up an oil lamp from a table beside the door and lit it. She followed him into the room and from the light of the lamp it was evident that a restoration project was in progress. There were a couple of saw horses, several stacks of boards, and two piles of river stones beside a massive fireplace along the back wall. The face of the fireplace was obviously being refurbished.

Faith watched Baxter grab a couple of logs from a bin on the hearth and set them atop the remains of a partially consumed one. He wadded some newspaper from a basket and retrieved a butane lighter from the mantle. After some coaxing the fire blazed brightly and Faith, with the blanket wrapped around her wet clothing, stepped to the hearth.

Baxter had not spoken since entering the house and neither had she. Was he angry because he'd had to venture into the storm to rescue her?

He reached for a poker hanging from a large hook embedded in the mortar of the fireplace and she studied his profile that appeared chiseled from stone. She cleared her throat. "I'm really sorry for causing all this trouble. I had no idea the storm would happen so fast. I thought I had plenty of time to take a walk because the clouds were so far away." She hesitated. "I don't know what else to say except that I'm stupid and really sorry."

Baxter replaced the poker and turned to gaze at her. His expression had softened and he puffed a breath. "You're not the first person to get stuck in a storm. We should have warned you that the weather can turn treacherous. It's rare, but days like this sometimes happen during summer."

The fire was beginning to blaze and Faith closed her eyes, willing her body to stop shivering. When she opened them again, Baxter was still watching her. Another shiver shook her, but it wasn't from the cold. She moved her attention to the fire. "How long do storms like this usually last?"

"They can continue for days."

Her eyes widened.

Baxter unexpectedly smiled. "But the weather report said it should only last a few hours. I expect we won't be here long."

Faith turned her back to the fire and glanced around the room. "Are you the one restoring Stone House?"

Baxter also turned around. "Yes. The work is being done by a contractor friend of mine who lives in town. He's been restoring the place during his off hours for the past three months, and now that I'm here for the summer, I'll be helping him"

Faith glanced around the room and the flickering shadows caused by the light of the fire and the oil lamp. "I guess there's no electricity."

"No. We're using that generator to power our tools." He pointed to a large object in a corner obscured by the shadows. "We'll be installing solar panels after the home is restored."

"After it's finished will you be opening the house to the public?"

"No. This is a pet project of mine. Since I was a child I've wanted to restore this place, and because my job is sometimes stressful, it's become a top priority. I want somewhere to kick back and experience, to some extent, what my forefathers did. Perhaps someday I'll open the home to guests at the B & B, but not now. We allow guests to wander the peninsula, but after the refurbishing is complete, this area will be off limits because I'm moving here from the B & B."

"Sounds lonely." Immediately, Faith wished she hadn't spoken. Somehow the words seemed to be a judgment call on her part. Obviously, Baxter liked solitude and it was none of her business. Thankfully, he ignored her comment.

"Would you like a tour?"

"Yes. Very much." She adjusted the

blanket and followed Baxter through an entry on the southern wall into the kitchen. As of yet, the room remained untouched and several cupboards had fallen to the ground. In one corner a fireplace smaller than the one in the other room had partially crumbled. Wooden countertops were decayed and the cast iron porcelain-enameled sink was pitted and chipped and hung precariously from its mooring. Along the western wall, which was the front of the house, a vintage coal and wood burning cook stove with a Great Majestic signet, was in better shape than anything else in the room. Faith walked to the antique and placed her hand on it. "This is magnificent and that brand is worth a fortune in the antiques' market. Are you planning to refurbish it?"

"Yes. Everything in the home that can be salvaged will be. Are you into antiques?"

"Not really. But I enjoy cooking and always wondered what baking on a stove such as this would be like."

"I expect the home will be finished around the end of summer, shortly before I return to California, and if you're still around, you're welcome to give the stove a go."

Surprised, she faced him. "Thank you." She hesitated before confiding, "I'm actually thinking about moving here. I'm…well…in a position to drastically change my lifestyle and…" Her voice trailed. "For years we…I've wanted to come here. You see, I have this coffee table book with photographs of wonderful small towns, and Somewhere was always my favorite." She turned back around and pretended to inspect the stove. Already she regretted having revealed so much about herself.

Baxter said softly, "I'll show you the rest of the house."

Thankful that he hadn't asked her questions about her background, they returned to the main room and one of two doors on the northern side of the cabin. It opened into a bedroom and he said, "The home has two bedrooms, the living area, and the kitchen. The outhouse was located about fifty feet behind the house, but that structure fell down years ago and the hole was filled in. The only modern improvements planned are a small bathroom with a shower at the rear of the kitchen, kitchen plumbing, and solar panels."

Faith asked, "Where does the water come from?"

"There's a well behind the house but right now it's capped. I have an engineer and architect coming next week to inspect it and design plans for the bathroom addition and kitchen piping. I'm not completely modernizing the home, although I may do that someday. For the foreseeable future I'll be using solar power for the refrigerator and a few kitchen appliances, also the water pump. The lighting will be from oil lamps. I'm installing a rainwater catchment system, too."

Faith followed him back to the living area that had quickly warmed and she returned to the fire. In response to his admission about not completely modernizing the house, she said, "I don't blame you for not modernizing. I visited Hope Museum and felt immersed in its history. It must be wonderful knowing your roots and growing up in such a lovely town."

Baxter chuckled. "That's true, but it's also true that everyone knows everyone's business. And gossip travels fast, whether it's true or not."

Faith smiled up at him. "I'm becoming a regular at Mama Pink's Diner so I can't disagree on that point." Suddenly, she realized that the wind was no longer howling or the thunder roaring.

Baxter said, "Sounds like the storm is over." He walked to the front door and opened it to a shaft of sunlight that bathed the center of the room, and for an instant, Faith forgot her sorrow and imagined a lovely family scene inside

Stone House.

13: Noah

Over the next two weeks Faith visited Vicky at the museum and also became friends with the boutique owner, Sandy Gutierrez. When Faith discovered that Vicky and Sandy were friends, she invited them both to dinner. After inquiring about the best seafood restaurant from Gabby, she was told that Seafood Heaven at the end of Ocean Boulevard, past the marina, served outstanding Italian and American cuisine. Gabby added without enthusiasm, "Even though Leonardo Constanzo owns it."

Faith's curiosity was piqued. "You're related, aren't you?"

Gabby grinned. "I hear you've been visiting Mama Pink's Diner, the gossip factory."

Faith felt terrible because Gabby's assessment was correct. Sheepishly, she replied, "I'm sorry. I was being nosy."

Gabby waved her apology aside. "Gossip that's not vicious is entertaining.

Yep, me and Leonardo go way back. He was married to my husband's second cousin, Loretta. He and I had a falling out years ago, but it would be petty of me to downgrade his restaurant when it's one of the finest around."

Although curious, Faith didn't broach the reason for the falling out, and Gabby didn't offer an explanation.

A couple of days later Faith picked Vicky up at the museum and followed her directions to Sandy's house on Hope Hill, behind Main Street. Her home was a tiny, adorable cottage surrounded by a white picket fence. Pink bougainvillea cascaded down porch rails and sea-lavender bordered the walkway to the porch steps, scenting the air with heady perfumes. On both sides of a bright red door, huge pots of strawberries spilled over their containers and mingled their fragrance with the other flower essences.

Sandy greeted the women with hugs and ushered them into a cottage as lovely inside, as out. Cherry red, pink, and lime green floral chairs faced a matching sofa, with a lime green oval rug spread between them on the shiny redwood floor. The colors were so cheery they could make anyone smile.

Immediately, Sandy invited Faith to view the rest of her home, which was just as colorful and cheerful as the living room. She winked at Faith, "Okay. Are you ready for my million dollar view?"

"I can't wait." Faith followed her new friend outside through the kitchen door and started ascending stairs to a roof deck. As soon as she glimpsed the view, she gasped. The sea and sky melded into one and she could see forever. So magnificent was the sight that she remained poised halfway up.

Behind her Sandy laughed. "Honey, I know it's wonderful, but you haven't even reached the top yet."

Faith quickly apologized and climbed the remaining stairs. Moving to the railing she gazed from north to south, from one jutting peninsula to the other, and then to the sea and beach between. She moved her gaze inland to Ocean Boulevard with its beautiful homes on either side of the street, and the marina at the end. Soon they would be dining at the restaurant hidden beyond the marina. She returned her gaze to Ocean Boulevard and followed the road until it reached Main Street, with Hope Bed & Breakfast on the northern corner. Beyond the B & B's private beach the sand met up with scattered boulders, and then the forested peninsula owned by Gabby. Faith searched for any glimpse of Stone House, but couldn't see it through the trees.

Dinner at Seafood Heaven was exquisite and possibly the best Faith had ever eaten. The restaurant's atmosphere was warm and inviting with large murals of seascapes depicting every aspect of ocean life, from dark storms whipping up frothy waves, to quiet beaches on sun drenched days. There were also depictions of fishermen hauling in bulging nets with the day's catch, and surfers riding huge waves. Above their table was a smaller mural of a lone island of waving palms set amidst shimmering blue water.

Faith couldn't remember a time since her family's deaths that she had enjoyed dining with friends. She listened to Sandy and Vicky joke about the latest debacle in town—Mama Pink tossing a rebellious teen out of her diner for loud and profane language, and then loudly lecturing everyone about common decency.

At the end of their meal when their waiter, a clean-cut young man with a winning smile who had been introduced as Leo's grandson, Noah, brought the check, Sandy and Vicky both tried to grab it, but Faith held it tightly. "No way. I invited you to dinner. This is my treat. I want—"

She was interrupted by a masculine voice behind her. "Actually, it's my treat." She turned to see Mr. Constanzo walking toward their table. He lifted the tab from her hand and grinned, and Both Sandy and Vicky greeted him cheerily. Faith started to protest his generosity, but Vicky said, "It's no use. Leo has a Santa Claus complex."

Faith graciously capitulated and Mr. Constanzo joined them. And when she expressed how much she'd enjoyed the meal and how great Noah was, he grinned. "Thank you. I'm very proud of my grandson. He could be running around with friends, but he chooses to work here. Sometimes I have to make him leave."

Vicky interjected, "Hmm. I wonder where he gets his work ethic?"

Leo laughed, glanced at Faith, and said, "I don't have a wine glass, but how about a toast to Faith, a woman who has charmed us with her quiet manner and sweet disposition."

Vicky lifted her half empty wine glass. "I second that."

Sandy lifted her empty one and chinked it to Vicky's. "And I third it."

14: Vee

After describing her evening with her new friends to Gabby, the gregarious lady invited Vicky and Sandy to dinner at the B & B the next week. As it turned out, most of the residents were out that evening, with only two elderly sisters from Tyler, Texas remaining for dinner. Everyone sat at one end of the table with Gabby in her usual place at the head, and Baxter, who generally sat at the other end, now beside his mother. Gabby patted the chair on the other side of her and motioned for Faith to sit directly across from Baxter.

At first, the conversation mostly praised the fabulous supper of pot roast, red potatoes and huge slices of onions, all simmered in delicious brown gravy, with side dishes of fried asparagus and sautéed mushrooms. Faith bit into a fluffy homemade biscuit while listening to Vicky mention the upcoming street fair and the booth she would be manning to promote

113

the museum. Sandy interjected that she also had a booth.

Baxter sipped his wine and asked Vicky, "Are you going to display any of your paintings at the booth? The ones showing different timelines are fantastic."

His question captured Faith's attention. She knew Vicky was artistic, but she didn't know she painted.

"No. I haven't painted for a few months, and although I love it, I've been experimenting with different mediums, the latest being clay sculpting." Vicky grinned. "And frankly I'm making a mess of it."

Suddenly, Faith remembered the paintings she'd seen at the local gallery with the artist's signature rendered simply as "Vee." She chanced a question. "Are your paintings in the gallery downtown?"

Vicky's grin widened. "Guilty."

"And do you sign them as Vee?"

"Guilty again."

Faith thought about the painting of the boy and dog. "Maybe you can tell me about the boy and dog. When I saw the painting I wondered if they lived here because I met the boy my first day in Somewhere. But I haven't seen him since then. He said his name is Owen and he was tossing a Frisbee for his dog. The Frisbee landed at my feet–" She stopped talking when Vicky's fork clattered to her plate. She glanced around the table. Everyone except for the sisters was looking at her like she'd grown two heads.

Vicky jumped to her feet and rushed from the room.

Faith looked at Gabby whose mouth was gaping and then glanced at Sandy whose eyes were bulging. She exclaimed, "What? What did I say?"

Baxter said, "Faith, may I speak with you in the other room?" Her gaze met his, and in his eyes she saw the same anger she'd initially witnessed the day he'd rescued her from the storm. His chair scraped the floor as he scooted it back. Faith glanced once more around the table and into the incredulous eyes of everyone except the sisters, who looked curiously from her to Baxter.

Faith's own chair sounded loud in the silent room as she pushed away from the table to follow him.

15: Accusation

Mystified, Faith followed Baxter into the library and he closed the door. He stepped to the fireplace mantel and slowly turned, but before he completely faced her, she said, "I have no idea what's going on or what I said that upset everyone."

Baxter stared at her for a moment and then replied with disdain, "Really?"

Faith didn't know how to answer his obvious contempt.

He continued, "And to think I was naive enough to make excuses for you during the storm, chalking it up to an overactive imagination and some gossip you'd heard."

Exasperated, she exclaimed, "What are you talking about?"

"I'm talking about Rex, as if you don't remember."

Searching her memory, Faith said, "You mean the child's voice calling for someone named Rex?"

Baxter crossed his arms over his chest and when he didn't change his sullen expression or angry stance, Faith turned to leave. She'd had enough of his game. Her hand was on the doorknob when he said, "Owen was Vicky's twin brother and his dog's name was Rex. They used to play Frisbee on the beach almost every day." His voice lowered. "And they've been dead for over twenty years."

Faith jerked her hand away from the door and whirled around. "That's not possible. I *saw* them. I *talked* to Owen."

Baxter's angry stance didn't budge. "You can stop playing your game now. If you're trying to build a reputation as a psychic, it's over. I ran the last so-called psychic out of town, and I'll do the same with you."

Faith's eyes widened. "I swear I've told you the truth. Maybe the part about hearing a child calling for Rex was part of the confusion of the storm, but I *talked* to a boy named Owen throwing a Frisbee for his dog."

Making an exasperated sound Baxter walked toward her, paused in front of her, reached around her to open the door, and said, "Vicky was very close to her brother and it took years for her to heal. Her mother and father never did. Her father deserted the family and her mother was institutionalized years ago." He shook his head. "Now I need to go undo your damage." He stepped around her.

Somehow Faith managed to return to her room without bursting into tears. As soon as she closed the door, however, she gulped back a wail. What had she done to Vicky? What had she done to all her new friends? Just when she'd decided that Somewhere was the place she could heal the sorrow in her own life, she had inadvertently caused fresh grief in another's. And now Baxter hated her. She had to leave town. Maybe she'd pack and leave tonight. She covered her face with her hands and quietly wept.

A soft knock startled her and she was

going to ignore it, but she heard Gabby say, "Faith, its Gabby. Can I come in? Please dear."

Inhaling a shuddering breath, she wiped her eyes. There was another knock and plea. Sniffing back tears, she stepped to the door and opened it a crack.

Gabby's expression turned from concern to relief. "Thank you for seeing me. Can I come in?"

Faith stepped aside.

Gabby entered and closed the door behind her. She motioned toward the small oak table. "May I sit?"

Faith nodded because she didn't trust her voice to speak.

Gabby said, "You sit, too, honey. We need to talk."

The lump in Faith's throat got so big she couldn't swallow and she wanted to run from the room. Instead, she sat across the table from Gabby.

Gabby unexpectedly reached to grasp Faith's hands. "I believe you, Faith. I believe you talked to Owen."

Faith gasped. "But Baxter said he's been dead for over twenty years. It had to have been a child with the same name, but your son thinks I'm trying to do something underhanded. I would never—"

"I know, dear, I know." Gabby squeezed Faith's hands. "Let me explain something about my son." She released their hands and leaned back in her chair. "We'll talk about Owen after I tell you about Baxter."

Faith remained silent but kept her gaze fixed on Gabby.

Puffing a breath, Gabby said, "Five years ago my son went through a divorce that devastated him. His wife was a master of disguise. If you'd met her you'd swear Baxter was the very reason for her existence. But she cheated on him, stole from him, and even aborted their child. He found out when she came to him demanding a divorce and saying she needed excitement in her life. It seems she'd met someone she thought could deliver what Baxter couldn't. He was shocked and when he refused, she dished out the dirty details of her double life. At first, he thought she'd had a mental breakdown, but after investigation, he discovered everything she'd said was true and even worse."

Faith's eyes widened.

"Oh, it gets dirty." Gabby sighed and continued, "Baxter refused to have a prenup believing he had married his soul mate, so Vanessa—that's her name—demanded an enormous settlement and threatened to draw out the divorce as long as it took to get what she wanted. Now mind you, I'm not saying my son was the perfect husband, but what she did was unconscionable. Vanessa brought him to his knees, financially and emotionally. It's only because he's a savvy investor that he's recovered most of what he lost monetarily in the divorce, but he's never recovered his emotional loss."

Gabby became silent while Faith

processed her revelation. After a time she said, "I know my son was hard on you, so that's why I exposed his history." She hesitated. "The other reason is because he's drawn to you. He really likes you. After I told him you're a widow I was under the impression he might ask you to dinner."

Jerking her gaze to Gabby's, Faith shook her head. "I don't think—"

"It's the truth. I know my son, and you're the first woman that's touched his heart since Vanessa." She made a dismissing motion with her hands. "But now we need to talk about Owen." Before Faith could say anything she said, "Owen was Baxter's childhood friend and after his death his mother and father started consulting psychics and paying them a lot of money. Psychics started coming out of the woodwork, which bankrupted the family. And when money ran out to pay the charlatans, they all left. Mrs. Patterson was always a little strange, but eventually she lost touch with reality when her husband abandoned her and Vicky. I suppose the séances in which Owen was supposedly contacted kept her mind intact, but when they stopped, she snapped." Gabby leaned forward and again held Faith's hands. "Three years ago we had a guest stay at the B & B and I could see that she was interested in Baxter. He, of course, was shying away from any relationship that involved commitment. At the time, we didn't know she was a psychic. One day, while she was sitting on the porch with Baxter and me, out of the blue she said, "I'm clairvoyant and there's a child named Owen who keeps visiting me with his dog."

Faith inhaled sharply.

Gabby also inhaled and released a long breath. "As you can imagine, Baxter was livid and delivered some choice words to our guest. The next day she left, but before she did, she spoke with me privately." Gabby stood and walked to the window while Faith waited to hear the conclusion to her incredible story. She pulled the curtain aside and stared outside. "She told me she didn't have ill feelings toward Baxter and that she understood his distrust because of his ex-wife's shenanigans." Gabby closed the curtain and turned around. "Now, mind you, no one had told her about Baxter's divorce. But then she changed the subject and said I needed to tell Vicky something that would be confirmed in three years."

Faith clasped her hand over her mouth.

"She said the message I should give his *twin* sister is that it wasn't her fault."

The women stared at each other for a long time and then Faith shook her head, disbelieving. "It has to be a coincidence or mistake. I simply met a boy named Owen who was vacationing with his family because–"

Gabby finished her sentence. "–because any other explanation is, well, impossible."

Faith nodded. "Exactly." She rubbed her clammy hands on her thighs. "I guess I should let you know I'm leaving tomorrow. I feel terrible about making Baxter angry and causing Vicky grief, so under the circumstances it would be better–"

"No! Baxter can get over himself, and as for Vicky, she needs a friend like you. I want you to stay."

"I can't come between you and your son."

"My son and I are always at odds, but that's what keeps us sharp, and, believe it or not, we enjoy our verbal sparring. His father and I did the same thing. If things got too comfortable between us, we looked for anything to debate. No, honey, you stay here." When Faith didn't respond, Gabby said softly, "There's another reason I think you should stay."

Faith questioned her with her eyes.

Gabby answered the nonverbal question. "You have sadness in you that's festered for a long time. When you

126

first got here it was an open sore, but over the past weeks it's started to scab over and heal. This town is good for you. You're making friends."

Swiping a tear, Faith replied, "But I probably lost them tonight."

The older woman grinned. "No, you didn't. Well, maybe my son. But he'll come around." She walked over and cupped Faith's cheeks. "At least stay until the end of summer. Don't make decisions based on what happened tonight. Granted, it's inexplicable, but let's see how summer plays out, and if you ever feel ready to confide in me about what broke your heart, I'm here for you."

Faith asked, "Are you going to tell Vicky what the clairvoyant told you?"

"No. Not yet. Something in my gut says to wait."

Faith was silent as she considered everything that had been revealed. "Okay, I'll stay, and tomorrow I'll go see Vicky and explain everything as coincidence."

"Good. And I'll tell my son to avoid you if he's going to be rude."

"I really hate that I upset him—"

"I don't." Gabby walked to the door, opened it, but turned around before leaving. "He needs a woman to upset him."

16: Frustration

Replacing the porch railing at Stone House, Baxter slammed his hammer against the nail until it was flush with the wood. He was furious with his mother.

"Hey Bax, if you keep hitting the nails like that, you're gonna split the wood. Why don't you use your nail gun?"

He slammed another nail. "Because I need to work off some frustration."

Brody Calhoun, the local carpenter who was restoring Stone House shot back, "That bad, huh?"

"Worse."

"Woman trouble?"

Baxter made a disgusted sound and pounded another nail.

"Want to talk about it?"

"Nope."

Brody shrugged and went back to using his nail gun.

After a few more nail poundings Baxter said, "The woman's a liar and my mother is defending her. You'd think a man's mother would be on his side, but not mine; she goes out of her way to make my life miserable." He wiped sweat from his forehead and glanced at his friend.

"You sure you don't want to talk about it?" Brody grinned.

Baxter rubbed his jaw and scratched his neck. "Brody, do you believe in supernatural shit?"

"You mean like aliens and spaceships?"

"No. Like ghosts."

"Hell, no. And I refuse to watch that crap on TV. Scares the shit outta me."

Baxter nodded. "Exactly."

"So, is your mom seeing ghosts?"

"No. But one of the B & B guests is." He paused. "At least that's what she claims, but I know it's a load of bull and I called her out on it."

Brody started reloading his nail gun. "So are you mad at your mother or the B & B guest?"

"Both. After I confronted the guest, I naturally thought she'd leave, but that was before my mom entered the picture and convinced her to stay."

Brody sat back on his heels. "Something I don't understand is why someone who thinks she saw a ghost makes you so mad. You got feelings for her?"

"Sweet Jesus, no. I got burned before by an angel-faced woman and I don't intend to make that mistake again. When I date I make sure the woman knows there are 'no strings' in our relationship." He made quote marks with his fingers.

"So, since you're off limits to all women, why has this one got you tangled in knots?"

"I'm not tangled—"

Brody cut him off with a disbelieving look.

Baxter cussed and went back to hammering.

Garnering her courage, Faith opened the door to the museum and stepped inside. Vicky glanced up from her desk

131

and smiled, but when she saw Faith her smile wavered. Before Vicky could speak, Faith said, "I'm really sorry about last night. I had no idea about your brother."

Vicky picked up a pencil and absentmindedly twirled it between her fingers. "Baxter was pretty harsh on you, wasn't he?"

Faith shrugged.

"It's only because we grew up together and he saw everything my family went through."

Faith said honestly, "I'm not angry with him. In fact, I was going to leave today, but Gabby talked me into staying."

Vicky laid the pencil down.

Since she wasn't sure how to broach the subject, Faith blurted, "The way I figure it, I talked to a boy who just happened to be named Owen and was playing with his dog. In fact, it's the only logical explanation. So, can we still be friends and forget what I said last night."

Vicky pushed away from her desk and walked over to Faith. "Yes. Let's forget about last night and I'm sorry about Baxter's reaction. I'll talk to him."

"No! I don't want to involve him anymore. I'll just go my way and he'll go his. We're adults and we can be civil. Promise you won't say anything to him."

Vicky frowned. "Okay. I won't say anything. I promise."

Later that day Faith returned to the art gallery and studied the picture of the child and dog.

17: Warning

Gabby sat on her front porch and lifted her needlepoint project onto her lap. Her disagreement that morning with Baxter had been refreshing. The way he kept carrying on about Faith was positive proof that he had feelings for her. Gabby knew her son. He was drawn to Faith physically and emotionally, and he was fighting it like it was World War III. She smiled.

A car slowed and entered the drive that ran to the parking lot at the rear of the house. Her smile faded. It was Leonardo Constanzo. She lifted a hand to smooth her hair and then jerked it back when her mind traveled thirty-seven years into the past. She put the brakes on any remembrances.

Methodically, she continued making cross stitches and stabbed her finger. "Damn!"

Leo rounded the path leading from the back to the front and paused at the porch steps. "Lovely day," he said.

"Yes. What brings you here, Leonardo?"

He started up the steps and corrected her, "That's Leo. We've known each other too long, *Gabriella.*" He grinned. "I mean Gabby."

Gabby felt the usual kick to her gut whenever Leo smiled and purposefully pricked her finger again.

He motioned to the wicker chair across from her. "May I?"

"And if I say no?"

His grinned widened. "I'll sit anyway." He folded his long, lean frame into the chair, which made Gabby aware of the extra pounds she carried, but usually didn't bother her.

"You're looking well," he said. "I always liked your hair in a French braid down your back."

Self consciously she brushed a wisp from her cheek and then berated herself. She wouldn't let Leo fluster her. Bluntly, she repeated, "Why are you here?"

Leo's chiseled features again broke into a smile. "I love a woman who speaks her mind."

Gabby frowned and waited for him to answer her question.

His smile vanished. "I've come to warn you about someone."

When he didn't continue, she said, "Who?"

"Me."

Her heart began thumping wildly.

He said seriously, "We've been dancing around each other for years and you know it. There's always been an attraction between us and that kiss years ago nailed it."

Anger made Gabby's heart pound even faster and she exclaimed, "I loved my husband–"

"And I loved my wife. That goes without saying. We both had wonderful marriages, but our spouses are dead, and we're alive." He leaned closer. "And we both know that kiss lit a spark between us that's never died, whether

136

you want to admit it or not."

Gabby began gathering her needlepoint. "I will not discuss this."

Leo reached a hand and placed it gently on her forearm. "I've been doing a lot of soul searching lately and I've come to the conclusion that I want you in my life Gabby, and not as a relative related by marriage."

Lifting her gaze from Leo's hand to his eyes she felt immobilized. His eyes were just as blue as in his youth; just as blue as the day he'd lowered his head to hers in the boathouse and kissed her with a passion she'd never forgotten." She jerked her arm away and abruptly stood. "It's not possible."

Before she entered the house he replied, "It is possible, and that's why I'm giving you fair warning that I'm out to win your heart once and for all."

18: Doris and Dave; Darren, Dirk, and Dog

The week after Baxter's confrontation Faith often found herself reconsidering her decision to stay in Somewhere, but every time she thought about leaving, it made her heart ache. So, after ten days, she did something crazy; she pulled out the business card Sandy had given her for real estate agents Doris and Dave McGovern and made an appointment.

On a cloudless Tuesday she drove to their office that was two streets off Main, and tried to appear businesslike, even though stepping out of her comfort zone had her heart thumping. She entered their office and a receptionist greeted her warmly, "Hello. Can I help you?"

"Yes. I have an appointment with Mr. and Mrs. McGovern. My name is Faith Bennison."

The young woman with wavy, shoulder-length hair that matched her flawless black complexion, smiled warmly. She was as beautiful as any contestant in a beauty pageant.

The receptionist said, "Welcome Faith. My name is Malana. I'll let the McGoverns know you're here. Can I get you some coffee, orange juice, soda, water?"

"Nothing, but thank you." Faith sat on the sofa across from the reception counter while Malana picked up the phone to announce her arrival. Glancing at the coffee table, she was pleasantly surprised to see the same tabletop picture book that had brought her to Somewhere. She smiled, picked it up, and turned to page ninety-two. *Is this a sign that I should move here permanently?* She heard a door open and footsteps in the hallway. Malana glanced up, smiled at her, and went back to typing. A moment later a large-boned black woman entered the waiting room with her hand extended. "Hello Ms. Bennison, or is it Mrs.?

Faith shook the woman's hand and

replied, "It's Mrs., although I'm a widow. Please call me Faith."

The woman gave her hand a squeeze. "I'm Doris McGovern, but call me Doris. My husband, Dave, got called out on an emergency and he'll meet up with us later. Come on back to my office so we can get acquainted."

Faith immediately liked Doris. She was just as friendly as Sandy had claimed. She followed the real estate agent down the hallway past four closed doors, two on each side, to a door at the end facing the hallway. Upon entering Doris' office, Faith was again impressed. It was light and airy, with pale yellow walls, aqua chairs, and several paintings reflecting the beauty of Somewhere. A long table behind the desk was placed under the only window in the room and held several framed photographs. Beyond the window an enclosed patio of profusely flowering hanging plants added charm and color to the setting.

Doris reached for a photograph. "This

is me and my husband on our thirty-eighth wedding anniversary, which was two years ago." She handed it to Faith.

In the picture Doris and a shorter man with fair skin and red hair, stood with their arms around each others' waists. Faith said, "It's a wonderful photo," and added uncharacteristically, "My husband and I would have been married eleven years in March." She noted sympathy in the other woman's eyes and said hastily, "The reason I'm here is because Sandy Gutierrez referred you, and I'm considering a permanent move to Somewhere."

Doris replaced the picture, motioned for Faith to sit, and then sat behind her desk. "I've lived in Somewhere since my marriage to Dave, who was born here." She smiled. "We met at a protest march in D.C. and it was love at first sight. My first day in Somewhere, I also fell in love with the town, and neither of us would leave for all the money in the world. So I can understand your desire to possibly relocate." She typed into her laptop. "I'll pull up all the listings in Somewhere. If you see anything of interest, I'd be happy to take you there. As a matter of fact, I'm yours for the day and lunch is on me." She pointed to a flat screen on her wall. "We just installed this monitor six months ago and it's great for showcasing properties." She then asked Faith about her preferred areas and preferences in a home.

Almost an hour later the women were saying goodbye to Malana and headed out the door. After they entered a Cadillac Escalade in the front parking lot, Doris said, "Malana is my granddaughter and she always spends summers with us. She lives in Denver and she'll be a senior this fall at the University of Colorado. Since childhood she's said, "Nana, I want to be just like you and Papa. I want to sell houses and live in Somewhere. Of course, we thought she would grow out of it, but she never has. Her mother and father insisted she attend the university, so she reached a compromise with them. She agreed to get a degree in business administration and then explore the job market, but if she still wanted to become a real estate broker after three years they would have to abide by her decision. And we said that if she chose that route, we'd teach her everything we know. So, I guess in four years we'll know her verdict."

Doris had talked nonstop and now she put the car in gear and drove out of the parking lot to enter street traffic. Since Faith had requested viewing houses on Hope Hill, she drove to a cross street and turned right, heading uphill. Their first stop was on Haven Drive, two-thirds of the way to the top. The home was a lovely two bedroom yellow cottage with white shutters and trim. The front of the house faced away from the ocean, but Doris said the view from the backyard was stunning. After walking through the twelve hundred square foot home that had been repainted inside and out and refurbished with maple cabinets and butcher block countertops, they stepped outside through the living room slider and onto the back terrace. The view was indeed stunning and similar to the one at Sandy's house. Faith walked across the yard to the fence that separated it from a home at a lower elevation.

Doris joined her and explained, "Since the homes are built on a hill, many of them are not as private as some people like. They were built back in the 1950s when city planning was more lax, and that's why your back yard abuts the one behind it."

Faith looked at the backyard of the other house that was strewn with children's toys and watched two boys playing in the dirt. Her heart wrenched and she blinked back tears. Her boy had loved playing in the dirt with his trucks. A large mixed breed dog happily circled and barked at the children. The dog saw her and ran to the fence, jumping against it. The boys turned and also ran to the fence. The younger one said, "Are you gonna be our neighbor?"

Faith swallowed the lump in her throat. "I'm not sure. I'm looking at several houses today."

Doris said, "Hello, Darren and Dirk."

The older boy said, "Hi, Mrs. McGovern."

The younger one asked, "Is Mr. McGovern with you?"

"No. He had business to take care of." She indicated Faith with a wave. "This is Mrs. Bennison."

The first boy said, "I'm Darren," pointed to the other child, "and he's my little brother Dirk." The dog barked. "And that's Dog."

Faith smiled. "His name is Dog?"

"Yep," Dirk said. "It's kinda a joke 'cause Dog is a dog."

Faith's smile widened. "I think it's a great joke."

Both boys grinned.

Doris asked, "Is your mother home?"

"No. We got a sitter. Mom got called to

work early."

Doris chatted with the children for a minute longer and then said, "We better be on our way. I have more houses to show Mrs. Bennison."

"Okay, but I hope you buy this one," said Darren and ran back to the dirt pile with Dirk. Dog jumped against the fence, barked, and then joined them.

While Doris was locking up the house, she said, "The boys' mother is a waitress at Mama Pink's Diner."

"Really? Maybe I've met her. What's her name?"

"Taylor Jones. She usually works the dinner shift so she can be home with her boys most of the day."

"I don't think I've met her."

"Then let's have lunch there and I'll introduce you."

19: Taylor

Faith entered Mama Pink's Diner with Doris who waved a greeting to Mama Pink. A few minutes after they were settled Mama came to their table to hand them menus. "Howdy, ladies! Good to see ya'll! Taylor will take your orders in a few minutes." She winked at Faith. "And since you're in the company of our local real estate agent, I'm guessin' you're in the market for a home in our lovely haven by the sea."

"I may be. Doris has shown me some beautiful properties."

The women chatted a little longer and then Mama said, "Can I get ya'll some coffee? I just perked a fresh pot."

"That sounds lovely," said Doris.

"Yes. I'll have some, too."

After Mama had served their coffees, a tall, slender brunette came to their table. She was dressed in jeans and the "uniform" of the diner, a pink T-shirt. Her hair was too short to be worn in a ponytail like the other waitresses, but the boyish cut was adorable.

Doris said, "Hi Taylor. I'd like you to meet Faith Bennison. I just showed her the house behind yours." She grinned. "And just to let you know, Dirk and Darren were in the backyard seeing how dirty they could get with Dog."

Taylor laughed. "I'm happy to meet you, Faith. Besides the dirt, I hope my boys were on their best behavior."

Although her heart hurt, Faith responded with a smile. "They were delightful." She wanted to say how much her own boy had loved playing in the dirt, but, of course, that would have brought her to tears.

New customers entered the diner and halted further small talk. Taylor said, "Our special today is roast beef and new potatoes and the vegetable of your choice. I'll be back in a few minutes to take your orders."

As Taylor walked away, Faith said, "What an incredibly beautiful woman and so personable."

Doris leaned in slightly. "She moved here about two years ago and everyone tells her she should be a model. Sandy even offered to put a portfolio together for her and represent her to some agencies in Portland and Seattle, but she wouldn't hear of it."

"Where did she move from?"

"No one knows because she doesn't talk about her past."

That surprised Faith, but before she could respond, Doris' cell phone beeped. She glanced at it and said, "It's a text from my husband. He needs to check on one of our properties on Ocean Boulevard and asks if we want to meet him there in an hour." She looked up. "Is that okay with you?"

"Oh, yes. In fact, I'd love to see a house on Ocean Boulevard. I've heard they're incredible."

"They certainly are, and this one is exceptional. It's selling for well over two million, but in my estimation, it's worth it."

When Taylor returned to their table, Faith ordered a BLT sandwich and Doris ordered shrimp salad with French bread. While Taylor took their orders, Faith marveled at her beauty and wondered at what age a woman was too old for a modeling career. Taylor was probably in her late twenties, but appeared to be much younger.

An hour later, Doris drove her Cadillac onto a circular drive and parked under a portico. Faith was impressed by the home and Doris glanced knowingly at her. "See what I mean about this house. And if you think the outside is gorgeous, wait until you step inside."

The front door opened and a red-headed, stocky man waved a greeting. Doris called, "Hi, honey." When they reached the door she said, "Dave, this is Faith Bennison." She turned to Faith. "Faith, my husband Dave."

They exchanged greetings and Faith expressed how impressed she was with the homes she'd seen so far. "Your wife has shown me wonderful properties so I have much to consider."

Dave said proudly, "Doris is an exceptional real estate woman." He stepped aside for them to enter the house. "Please come in. We're holding an open house tomorrow and I had to make sure everything is in order. I hope you don't mind being waylaid, Faith."

"Not at all. In fact, I'm in awe of the homes on Ocean Boulevard."

"And this is one of the finest. It's not as large as some, but what it lacks in interior space, it makes up for in outdoor space. The great room and the master suite have automatic glass pocket doors that open the entire length of their rooms. Come on, I'll give you the tour."

Faith followed the real estate agents through a large marble foyer into the great room and exclaimed, "It's magnificent. I feel like I'm outside."

Dave said, "Watch this," and walked to a touchscreen on the wall next to the glass. He tapped it and the windows instantly turned opaque. "It's called SmartGlass and makes the room invisible to the outside. Quite ingenious." He brought the windows back to transparency and touched the screen again. From the center, the pocket doors began retreating to each side.

Faith was impressed and followed Doris outside onto a huge flagstone terrace with fire pit, outdoor kitchen for barbeques, colorful patio furniture arranged in klatches, hot tub and lap pool. It was luxury in the extreme. Beyond a natural stone barrier, waves pounded the shore less than a hundred feet away.

Doris said, "The beach along this stretch is private to the homeowners of Ocean Boulevard. Can you imagine waking up to this every morning?"

Faith sighed. "It would be incredible. Whoever buys this home is buying a piece of heaven."

20: Outdoor Market

A week later, on Saturday, the first day of the street fair, Faith dressed in comfortable beige slacks and a sleeveless blue blouse. She chose dangly sky blue earrings to match her blouse, but decided to forego the long matching necklace since she would be helping Vicky at the museum booth. She grabbed a sweet roll from a basket on the table and poured coffee into a to-go cup. She was going to meet her friend at the museum at eight.

In the kitchen she could hear the Piersons laughing and preparing breakfast. They were a wonderful family and Faith often felt guilty for not warming up to Jennie's overtures of friendship, but the thought of spending time with her and hearing about her husband and boys, was too much for Faith at this time. She knew she was being selfish, but she just wasn't ready.

Gabby bustled into the room carrying a

vase of yellow roses and set it in the center of the table. In her rapid fire manner of speaking, she said, "Good morning, Faith. My flower garden is terrific this year. I guess you're off to help Vicky."

Faith smiled. "Yes, and I'm looking forward to it."

"Good. It'll get you used to being a part of the community."

Faith didn't respond. Although she had toured a few more homes with Doris, she was still vacillating about a permanent move to Somewhere. Oh, she loved the town and the ocean and the townsfolk, but Baxter's distrust of her motives bothered her. She knew she should dismiss his avoidance and cool demeanor, but it hurt. Was she ready to settle down in a place where she already had a strike against her from one of the natives? Was she waiting for a sign? She said, "These sweet rolls are delicious. Did the Piersons bake them?"

"Oh no, dear. I learned that recipe

from Mrs. Lucky. She and her husband owned Mr. Lucky's Grocery."

Her words triggered something in Faith's memory that Owen had said. A chill raced up her spine. "Owned? Is the store no longer there?"

"Goodness, Mr. and Mrs. Lucky died years ago and the property has been sold a couple of times since then. Right now it's a print shop."

Faith felt faint.

Gabby stepped closer. "What's wrong, Faith? You look like you've just seen a ghost."

Faith pulled out a chair and slowly lowered herself into it. With a concerned expression, Gabby pulled out the chair next to her and sat down. "Tell me what's wrong?"

Inhaling a couple of times, Faith whispered, "The boy at the beach, Owen, told me that you baked cookies and sold them at Mr. Lucky's Grocery. He said he worked there after school helping Mr. Lucky stock shelves. He said he loved your cookies."

Gabby gasped and placed her hands over her mouth. "Oh, my God, that's true."

Faith met her gaze and rasped, "What's going on?"

An hour later Faith was helping Vicky set up shop under a canopy that had already been erected by Mr. Constanzo. As she set out flyers and brochures, she couldn't stop thinking about the revelation Gabby had dumped on her. Was someone playing a sick joke on them? Since she refused to believe she'd had a conversation with a boy who had been dead for more than twenty years, what other explanation was there? She wanted to ask Vicky about her twin brother, but considering how upset she'd been when Faith unwittingly mentioned his name before, that wasn't an option.

Forcing herself to quell her ponderings and questions, she focused on helping at the booth. Soon, the entire downtown was filled with tourists and locals. The atmosphere became festive and joyful and Faith found herself exuberantly handing out brochures and inviting people to the museum. Around mid morning Mr. Constanzo visited the booth and thanked them for their hard work. "I've seen lots of people carrying the new brochures. Good job, ladies."

Faith said, "Your museum is amazing and I'm happy to let people know about it."

While Vicky and Leo spoke about business matters, Faith let her gaze wander among the crowd. Unexpectedly, she saw something that caused the hair on her neck to stand up. Disappearing around a booth several yards away was a boy wearing a blue ball cap followed by a large red dog. Faith made a choking sound and Vicky and Leo stopped talking to glance at her. She was already heading out of the booth and called over her shoulder, "Excuse me. I'll be right back."

Rushing toward the place where the boy and dog had been, she glanced in every direction, but didn't see them. *Damn.* Turning to Art in his booth she said, "Did you just see a boy in a ball cap walk this way?" She purposefully didn't mention the red dog for obvious reasons.

"No. I didn't see a child. Did you lose one?"

The truthful answer was yes because her son had died. "No. I..." While she struggled to finish her sentence she glanced past Art into his booth and saw a painting that made her forget her train of thought. It was the painting of Owen and his dog.

The owner turned to see what she was staring at and when he turned back around, he said, "That painting was done by a local. Her name is Vicky Patterson and she runs the museum."

"Yes, I've met her and we've become friends."

"Ah." He hesitated. "So you know the history behind this painting?"

"I understand that the boy's name was Owen and he drowned when he was nine. I heard he was last seen tossing a Frisbee for his dog, but a day later his body and the dog's washed ashore below Stone House. No one is exactly sure what happened but the loss devastated his family."

"Yep, that's the crux of it."

Faith stared at Owen in the painting. "I'd like to buy the picture. Will you hold it at the gallery until I can bring you a check and pick it up tomorrow?"

The proprietor's expression held both surprise and pleasure. "Of course. I'll even give you a gift certificate for fifty dollars off another purchase at my gallery when you're ready."

"Thank you. How long has the painting been hanging there?"

With a sheepish expression, he replied, "Three years."

"Three years! But it's so good."

"I know. Vicky's other paintings usually sell within weeks." He shrugged. "I guess this one's been waiting for you."

Faith gave him a startled glance and said, "Because of the sorrow surrounding this picture, I'd appreciate it if you didn't tell Vicky I'm the one purchasing it."

Art looked mildly intrigued, but didn't pursue further questions. "Not a problem."

During the remainder of the day Faith and Vicky took turns watching the booth so they each had time to explore the outdoor market. Vicky had urged Faith to leave for the day, but Faith adamantly refused. She wasn't about to abandon her new friend to hoards of visitors. Throughout the day several locals stopped by to chat. Gabby and Mama Pink were together. Sandy was alone. Taylor was with her sons and three other boys. She introduced the children and said they were neighbors, and Faith's heart did its usual dive. The home she adored was surrounded by boys around the same age her son would have been.

On the heels of Taylor's visit, Jennie

and James showed up with their boys. Immediately after they left, Baxter approached their booth. He moved his gaze from Vicky to Faith, and back. Since his confrontation, they hadn't spoken more than a few sentences, and Faith wondered what he'd say if she admitted to seeing a boy and dog today that resembled Owen and Rex, and that she'd purchased Vicky's painting. She had no doubt his accusations would continue.

Baxter spoke with Vicky for a few minutes and then said, "Faith, did you get a chance to explore the market?"

She was surprised by his address and stuttered, "Y-yes. Vicky and I took turns watching the booth."

"Did you try out the deep fried pickles?" A smile tilted one side of his mouth.

The smile took her off guard and she stammered again. "N-no." She hated being tongue-tied.

Baxter moved his gaze to Vicky. "Would you mind if I stole Faith away for a while. A day at Somewhere's Annual Street Festival isn't complete without a deep fried pickle.

Vicky grinned. "I agree." She gave Faith a little push. "Off with you."

As Faith stepped out of the booth, Baxter said to Vicky, "I'll bring a pickle back for you."

"Thanks, Baxter."

Baxter held Faith's elbow as he guided her through the throng of pedestrians. Over the past few days his anger had quelled and he felt guilty about the way he'd spoken to a guest of the B & B. She hadn't retaliated in any way and continued to be soft-spoken and pleasant to everyone. If she was a charlatan, she was excellent at covering it up. Her encounter with a boy named Owen and his dog, and later possibly hearing a child call for Rex at Stone House, made no sense, but he was tired of feeling animosity toward her. In fact, he was tired of feeling animosity toward his ex-wife.

His mother was right; he needed to move beyond his past, and maybe Faith needed to move beyond hers, too.

They reached the pickle vender and stood at the back of the line. He cleared his throat. "I'd like to apologize for my behavior. I was horribly rude to you and it was uncalled for. Faith lifted her expressive chocolate eyes to his and his heart jumped.

She spoke so softly that he leaned forward to hear. "I'm really sorry about upsetting you. And I must confess that I don't understand what's happened. In fact, I've racked my brain to the point of migraines trying—"

He touched his index finger to her lips. "You're not the one to blame; I am. Will you have dinner with me tomorrow night?" Her eyes widened slightly before she glanced away. He could tell she was nervous. When she again met his gaze, he said, "My mother told me you're a widow, or I wouldn't ask."

She continued staring into his eyes,

apparently trying to judge his motive, and finally said, "All right."

The vendor shouted, "Next!"

21: Dinner

Faith grabbed a pair of scissors and shortened the strand of hair that was giving her fits. Dampening it and twirling it around her finger, she hoped it would look wispy when it dried. She left the bathroom and sat on the side of her bed, willing the butterflies in her stomach to fly away. She should have refused the dinner invitation from Baxter, but he'd seemed so sincere in his apology and his eyes had been so blue, she'd been unable to turn him down. In half an hour she would meet him downstairs.

Her gaze shifted to the wrapped painting of Owen purchased at the street fair. No one knew she had it except the art proprietor. She considered unwrapping it, but discarded that thought. She wasn't ready to ponder the strange happenings since arriving in Somewhere. So, instead of twiddling her thumbs for thirty minutes, she decided to continue writing the pirate story she'd been composing since her first foray into the woods. She sat at her desk and opened her laptop. Her hero was a ruthless pirate named Dax who looked like Baxter. She tapped a finger against her chin and decided to improve his moral fiber, and since she was about to send him into the midst of battle with an English clipper ship, what better way than to add chivalry. So engrossed was she in writing a scene between Dax and a widowed Duchess named Lady Charity, that she forgot about the time until there was a knock on her door. Baxter called, "Faith? Are you in there?"

She jumped up and rushed to open the door. "I'm so sorry! I got ready early and then decided to pass the time by working on a story I'm writing."

She wished she could take the words back when he glanced past her to the desk and said, "So you like to write? You can tell me all about it during dinner."

Faith felt her face flame. She could never tell Baxter he was the dashing Dax in her novel. She returned to her desk. "Just let me power my laptop down and then we can go."

An hour later while they conversed over Crab Louie at Seafood Heaven, Baxter lifted his wine glass. "A toast to whatever you're writing and may it be enjoyed by many."

Faith had no choice but to lift her glass and touch it to his. She was about to change the subject when he said, "So are you writing poetry, fiction, nonfiction?"

"Ah, fiction."

He grinned. "Judging by the way you're blushing, I'm wondering if you write romance."

"I-I actually have some children's stories in mind," she replied inanely.

"But this one isn't for children?"

She gulped her Chardonnay. "No. It's...I guess I should admit its romance." She lifted her gaze to his.

He was grinning. "My mother loves romance books. You'll have to let her read it when you finish."

Faith had no inclination to let anyone read her story. It was simply a form of distraction. Instead of admitting that, she said, "It's amateurish and I'd be embarrassed for anyone to read it."

Their waiter returned to check on them and after he left Faith quickly changed the conversation. "I understand the owner of this restaurant is a relative of yours."

"Only by marriage. He was married to the granddaughter of Randall Hope. Leo is a nice guy and we get along great. My mother, however, not so much."

Faith wanted to ask him why and her expression must have revealed that, because Baxter laughed and said, "The whole town knows they don't get along, but no one knows exactly why, although there are many speculations." He grinned. "But just like the speculations of Stone House being haunted, it adds mystery to our town."

Their conversation during the remainder of the meal was pleasant and interesting and she learned that Baxter was a software engineer who worked via the internet and also dabbled in investments, which explained his ability to spend summers in Somewhere. She was curious as to why he didn't live there permanently, but didn't ask. As for herself, the only thing she revealed was that she had been an elementary school teacher. Then she related funny stories about her students.

They were pleasantly interrupted when a dessert cart featuring assorted mouth-watering pastries and puddings was pushed to their table by Leo Constanzo. He and Baxter shook hands and exchanged pleasantries, and then Leo shifted his attention to Faith. "Thank you again for helping Vicky at the festival. She calculated that over two hundred flyers were passed out and I expect there will be an increase in customers tomorrow and the rest of the week."

"It was fun and made me feel a part of something." As soon as Faith said the words, she wanted to take them back.

She was sure they made her appear lonely and pitiful, and the last thing she wanted was for anyone to feel sorry for her, especially Baxter.

Leo said, "Well, I heard through the grapevine that Doris and Dave are showing you homes in Somewhere, so maybe you're already a part of the community."

Faith didn't want to continue the direction of their conversation because, inevitably, it would lead to questions about why she was relocating. She moved her gaze to the dessert cart and pointed to one. "Is that tiramisu?" The conversation was effectively changed.

By the time Faith finished her chocolate crumble tiramisu and dessert wine, she was stuffed. She hadn't eaten so much in years, but every bite had been delicious. She leaned back in her chair. "Baxter, the meal was fabulous. Thank you for bringing me here."

"Thank you for accepting my invitation. I haven't enjoyed myself so much in, well, years."

Faith was surprised by his admission.

22: Problem

When Gabby learned that her son had taken Faith to dinner, she was ecstatic, but careful not to show it. "So, I hope you apologized to Faith for your rude behavior about Owen."

Baxter glanced up from typing into his laptop and replied dryly, "Do you really think I need to answer that?"

She grinned and plopped across the couch. "No. I know you were a perfect gentleman and *profusely* apologetic. So, tell me about your date. Unless you took her out of town, I'm guessing you went to Seafood Heaven." She wrinkled her nose, not because the restaurant wasn't fabulous, but because it was owned by Leo. She thought about his recent visit when he'd suggested that she was suppressing romantic feelings for him, and then remembered their kiss from years ago. She wouldn't think about that.

Baxter said, "Mom, what is it with you and Leo. He's a nice guy and you've known him for years. What's this aversion you have to him?" He stretched and grinned. "Do you secretly have a crush on him and think it would make dad turn over in his grave?"

Gabby jumped to her feet. "I do not! And I think that's a terrible thing to say!"

Clearly taken aback, Baxter frowned and lifted his hands in surrender. "I was only kidding."

Gabby sat back on the couch and diverted the conversation. "I'm waiting to hear about your date."

"Don't try to make something out of it. We just had dinner."

"Did she share anything about herself?"

"She admitted that the McGoverns are showing her homes for sale and reiterated how much she likes Somewhere. She also said she once taught third graders. That's about it."

Gabby placed her elbows on her knees and cupped her chin. "That woman needs to unburden herself and what better person than you—a jilted husband. Maybe the two of you can overcome life's challenges together."

Baxter choked on his iced tea. "Mother! Now *you're* the one saying terrible things!"

"Yes, but it's true." She rose to leave, but when she reached the door, she glanced over her shoulder. "If ever there was a match made in heaven, it's the two of you." Baxter glared at her, but before he could reply, she shut the door.

Later that day, while pulling weeds in the vegetable garden on the kitchen side of the house, she heard a car pull to the curb. Rising slowly from a kneeling position because her knees sometimes gave her trouble, she brushed her dirty hands on her smock and walked to the front of the house. Leo had just stepped onto the pathway and when he saw her, he paused. She wanted to duck behind the house to avoid him, but it was too late. He stepped off the path and walked toward her. "Hello Gabby. Nice day."

She put her hands in the pockets of her smock. "Yes. They usually are during summer." He stopped in front of her and his gaze made her heart lurch.

"I need to talk to you about something." His tone was serious.

"If it's about what you said last time you were here, I want you to leave."

He shook his head. "You're off the hook for now."

She motioned toward the porch. "Okay. Have a seat and I'll wash up and bring us tea." She stepped past him.

"Wait."

She paused and turned around and he reached to gently rub his thumb across her cheek. "You're smudged with dirt."

Gabby couldn't remove her gaze from his and felt the same electricity that had zinged between them so many years ago. She ducked her head. "Like I said, I'll wash up and join you on the porch."

Inside the house she rushed upstairs to her bathroom and stared in the mirror. The eyes reflecting back sparkled and the cheeks were flushed. *Damn.* Angrily she splashed water on her face, pulled out the large clip holding her hair in a knot at the nape of her neck, and jerked a brush through her tresses before twisting it back into a knot. She removed her smock, considered changing into a fresh blouse, and cursed again. She wouldn't try to look nice for Leo.

After she left her room she headed for the kitchen to pour two glasses of iced tea, and to prolong the moment before having to see Leo again, she complimented J & J on the Mexican meal they had served the night before. Then she gulped a breath and returned to the porch.

Leo was talking on his cell phone. "Noah, replace the merlot with our most expensive cabernet. We need to keep some merlot in reserve." He glanced at her. "Gotta go. I'll talk to you later, son."

Gabby handed Leo his tea as he pocketed his phone. "How is Noah? I haven't seen him lately."

"He's working his tail off at the restaurant and marina and hates that I'm insisting he attend Portland University after he graduates next year. He keeps telling me he wants to follow in my footsteps, and I keep telling him he has to explore his options." He blew a breath. "It's not that I'm opposed to him taking over the reins of my businesses someday, I just want him to be sure that's what he really wants. It's the same problem Dave and Doris are having with Malana." He shrugged. "Are we wrong in asking our children to explore the world when they insist they want to live and work in Somewhere?" His gaze drifted across the street. "Maybe Baxter is the exception. I always thought he'd get tired of city living and return to help you with the B & B, but he hasn't."

Gabby glanced at her hands. "That's what I thought too, but his wife messed up his head." Realizing she was speaking too intimately with Leo, she said matter-of-factly, "So, what is it you want to talk about?"

Leo moved his gaze from staring at the park across the street to staring in her eyes. "Somewhere has a problem, which means we have a problem."

23: Collision

Baxter watched his mother throughout dinner and knew something was wrong. Although she spoke with animation to their guests, it was forced, and he wondered what had happened between her playful goading that morning and now.

Faith wasn't at the table because she'd said she was dining with Vicky and Sandy, and he missed her. He made polite conversation with their guests, answered their questions, and talked about local attractions, all the while impatient for dinner to be over so he could question his mother.

Several guests retired to the library for dessert and Baxter felt obligated to join them. His mother declined with the excuse that she had to prepare menus for the next week. Baxter knew she was stretching the truth and let her know by his expression.

Finally, the guests retired to their

rooms and he escaped upstairs. When he entered the sitting room his mother was on the floor in front of the coffee table shuffling through papers strewn across it. She was wearing her reading glasses and glanced up with a worried expression.

"Mother, what the hell is going on?"

She straightened and leaned back against the couch. "Leo stopped by today to deliver some bad news." She glanced at the coffee table.

Baxter sat on a chair across from the couch. "I'm listening."

"As you know, when Oliver Hope divided up Hope Cove, he left the northern end to his son, Sebastian, and the southern to his son, Randall, which through inheritance has resulted in Leo owning the southern portion and me the northern. As for the land in between, he gave it to the town with the city council having governing power. And, for years, that's worked just fine because the council has protected our town from corporate takeovers."

Baxter nodded. "Okay. So what's happened that has you and Leo so concerned?"

Gabby balled her hands into fists and said with conviction, "I love this town!"

Rather than force her to continue, Baxter waited.

Finally, she said, "Because you're gone most of the year, I'm not sure if you're aware that two new council members were elected six months ago. Before then, like always, the council wanted to keep big business out of our town, but I just discovered that the dynamics changed with the new members." She stopped speaking long enough to inhale. "Leo stopped by to tell me that Henry Ward, our longstanding board member, privately came to him with a heads up about a corporation wanting to negotiate the purchase of a portion of the public beach. They said they wanted to build a resort that would 'substantially increase our tourist base'."

She made air quote marks and stared at her son. "And you know what that means."

Baxter blew a breath. "Yeah. It means Somewhere will become a huge tourist destination and other corporations will want to buy up downtown and put our small shops out of business. And our quaint town will disappear altogether." He glanced at the paperwork on the table.

Gabby waved her hand over it. "These are copies of the original documents dividing the property into the three sections. I was reading through them to see if there were any clauses that might throw a monkey wrench into selling part of the beach for commercial purposes."

"And?"

"So far I haven't found anything. Maybe you'll give it a go."

"Of course I will. I don't want Somewhere to become another cash cow for corporate swindlers. The only reason the town sold lots in the eighties was because it was going broke. We've been fiscally sound since then." He leaned forward and placed his hands on his knees. "This stinks."

Gabby started gathering the paperwork. "Yeah, to high heaven."

The next day Baxter read through the documents and could find no loophole, and by midmorning he was angry and frustrated. As his mother had pointed out, he was gone most of the year, but Somewhere was his home and the place he wanted to retire when the time came. He loved the relaxed atmosphere, the friendly townspeople he'd known all of his life, the quaint town, and the inherent beauty of the land.

After reading the documents he called Leo to discuss the situation and ask him to also read the paperwork. Leo said, "The first thing I did was pull out my copy. I couldn't find anything either so I gave it to my attorney. It didn't take him long to call and say there was nothing we could use."

"Damn."

Leo's tone was reassuring when he said, "Nothing's been finalized and it may never happen, but if the ball starts rolling in the wrong direction there's an incredible attorney in Portland I'm going to hire to fight this."

"Good. Just let me know and I'll pay my share of the expense."

"Thanks, Baxter." He hesitated. "How's your mother taking this? She was pretty disturbed, especially when I told her the location of the resort would be close to the B & B."

"She's upset, of course, but she's a tough cookie. We'll get through it."

There was silence and then Leo said, "What I didn't tell her is that the proposed resort would be four stories high and block her view of the beach beyond."

Baxter blasted out another profanity.

Leo responded, "I couldn't have said it better."

"Let's keep that part to ourselves for the time being," Baxter cautioned.

"I agree."

By the time Baxter hung up from speaking with Leo, he was livid. Jerking his sunglasses on and grabbing a water bottle from the fridge, he set out for Stone House. Maybe the walk would help his disposition.

By the time he reached the fork his overactive imagination was envisioning hoards of tourists overrunning his part of the cove. Blindly continuing along the western trail he rounded a tree and crashed into Faith. She yelped and he had to do some fancy footwork to keep them both from toppling to the ground. By the time he'd stabilized them, he was holding her tightly against his chest with his arms splayed across her back. She pushed against his chest and gasped, "Baxter!"

He stepped back and moved his hands to her shoulders. "Faith, I'm so sorry! I wasn't paying attention! Are you hurt?"

"No. No. You just surprised me."

They stared at each other until he

became aware that he was still holding her shoulders. He released her. There was an awkward silence and then he said, "I was on my way to Stone House to check on its progress. Looks like you're headed there, too. Mind if I join you?"

"Of course not."

He started to hold her elbow while they walked, but decided against it. Her body against his had felt wonderful and now he wanted to kiss her. To make conversation he said, "The weather is certainly different from the last time we were here."

She laughed softly and lifted her head to look at him. "What? You mean no torrential downpour, blinding lightening, deafening thunder; stuff like that?"

He grinned. "Speaking of adjectives, how's your fantastic romance story coming along?"

She quickly returned her gaze forward. "Oh, I'm still working out the plot and characters."

When she didn't say more, he said, "Can you give me a hint about the plot?"

By the time Baxter hung up from speaking with Leo, he was livid. Jerking his sunglasses on and grabbing a water bottle from the fridge, he set out for Stone House. Maybe the walk would help his disposition.

By the time he reached the fork his overactive imagination was envisioning hoards of tourists overrunning his part of the cove. Blindly continuing along the western trail he rounded a tree and crashed into Faith. She yelped and he had to do some fancy footwork to keep them both from toppling to the ground. By the time he'd stabilized them, he was holding her tightly against his chest with his arms splayed across her back. She pushed against his chest and gasped, "Baxter!"

He stepped back and moved his hands to her shoulders. "Faith, I'm so sorry! I wasn't paying attention! Are you hurt?"

"No. No. You just surprised me."

They stared at each other until he

became aware that he was still holding her shoulders. He released her. There was an awkward silence and then he said, "I was on my way to Stone House to check on its progress. Looks like you're headed there, too. Mind if I join you?"

"Of course not."

He started to hold her elbow while they walked, but decided against it. Her body against his had felt wonderful and now he wanted to kiss her. To make conversation he said, "The weather is certainly different from the last time we were here."

She laughed softly and lifted her head to look at him. "What? You mean no torrential downpour, blinding lightening, deafening thunder; stuff like that?"

He grinned. "Speaking of adjectives, how's your fantastic romance story coming along?"

She quickly returned her gaze forward. "Oh, I'm still working out the plot and characters."

When she didn't say more, he said, "Can you give me a hint about the plot?"

186

By the time Baxter hung up from speaking with Leo, he was livid. Jerking his sunglasses on and grabbing a water bottle from the fridge, he set out for Stone House. Maybe the walk would help his disposition.

By the time he reached the fork his overactive imagination was envisioning hoards of tourists overrunning his part of the cove. Blindly continuing along the western trail he rounded a tree and crashed into Faith. She yelped and he had to do some fancy footwork to keep them both from toppling to the ground. By the time he'd stabilized them, he was holding her tightly against his chest with his arms splayed across her back. She pushed against his chest and gasped, "Baxter!"

He stepped back and moved his hands to her shoulders. "Faith, I'm so sorry! I wasn't paying attention! Are you hurt?"

"No. No. You just surprised me."

They stared at each other until he

became aware that he was still holding her shoulders. He released her. There was an awkward silence and then he said, "I was on my way to Stone House to check on its progress. Looks like you're headed there, too. Mind if I join you?"

"Of course not."

He started to hold her elbow while they walked, but decided against it. Her body against his had felt wonderful and now he wanted to kiss her. To make conversation he said, "The weather is certainly different from the last time we were here."

She laughed softly and lifted her head to look at him. "What? You mean no torrential downpour, blinding lightening, deafening thunder; stuff like that?"

He grinned. "Speaking of adjectives, how's your fantastic romance story coming along?"

She quickly returned her gaze forward. "Oh, I'm still working out the plot and characters."

When she didn't say more, he said, "Can you give me a hint about the plot?"

"Ah, it's an adventure."

Baxter stopped walking. "Okay, Faith. You have me on pins and needles. Can you tell me *anything* substantial? I'm really interested."

She blushed. "I'm not a good writer. I'm just doing this for therapy. But…but…the hero is a pirate."

He grinned again. "I have a feeling you're a very good writer, but I won't press you for more information." His grin widened. "At least for now."

They continued walking and he wondered what she'd meant about the writing being for therapy. Therapy for what? He'd bet the farm it had something to do with her being a widow.

Faith stepped onto the porch of Stone House and released a sigh. She hoped Baxter wouldn't ask questions about her pirate story. If he found out he was the inspiration for her swashbuckling hero/villain, she would be mortified. Maybe she should trash the project, but the thought of doing so made her indescribably sad. No, she would continue writing until...what? It was finished and she no longer needed the distraction? Baxter left in the fall? She lost interest in the tale? She had no idea. The only thing she knew right now was that she needed to write. Her faux pas of admitting to Baxter that it was for therapy had slipped out, but thankfully he hadn't seemed to pick up on it.

Baxter unlocked the front door and stepped inside to light the lantern. He held the lamp high. "So, what do you think?"

She could see that much had been accomplished and walked to the fireplace to smooth a hand over the rough hewn spruce log that was the mantle, and then down the river stones making up the face. The firebox had been cleaned out and fresh logs were on the iron grate. "It's certainly changed. The fireplace looks awesome."

Baxter followed her and also

smoothed a hand down the stones. "I'm very happy with it."

"What about the kitchen? Is it finished?"

"No, but it soon will be. Come on. I'll show you."

Faith entered the kitchen and turned in a circle. The room was fantastic! The wooden countertops were restored and the fireplace, although smaller than the one in the main room, was just as magnificent. A cauldron hung over the firebox and Faith envisioned the many wonderful soups that must have been prepared there.

Baxter said, "A penny for your thoughts."

Smiling, she replied, "I was imagining a huge pot of clam chowder simmering in the fireplace."

Baxter returned her smile and said softly, "Maybe someday we'll have to make that a reality."

Unexpectedly, Faith heard a dog bark, which in and of itself wasn't unusual, but then she heard a boy calling, "Rex! Over here!" She gasped and placed a hand over her throat. "Did you hear that?"

Baxter's brow furrowed as he watched her. "Hear what?"

When she didn't answer, he asked, "Are you all right?"

Faith wanted to tell him she'd just heard Owen calling for his dog, but she knew that would finish their tentative truce and budding friendship. Instead, she tried to compose herself. "Oh, nothing, I'm just–"

"Rex! Over here!" The voice sounded like it was just outside the house and Faith stared at Baxter. Then the dog barked again. Surely, he had heard it, but nothing in his expression registered that he had.

"Rex! Rex!" The voice sounded so near that she squealed and jumped into Baxter's arms. She clung to him and buried her face in his chest. His arms went around her and he lowered his head to her ear.

190

"Faith, what's wrong?"

"I-I'm not sure. I think the death of my son is making me hear things."

He tightened his hold and became her lifeline to sanity. Finally, when her heartbeat slowed and her breathing quieted, he moved his hands to her shoulders and stepped back. "Faith, look at me."

She lifted her head and inhaled a shuddering breath.

"Honey, would you feel better if you talked about whatever's bothering you?"

She couldn't remove her gaze from his and longed to finally share her pain with someone. Slowly, she nodded, but nothing came out when she tried to speak. He placed a finger over her lips. "Shh." Reaching an arm under her knees he lifted and carried her back to the main room, and she apprehensively glanced around, but there was no child or dog there. He sat on the fireplace hearth and settled her on his lap. She snuggled her head beneath his chin and burrowed closer into his warmth. He made her feel safe.

After a long time she said, "My husband and son died three years ago." She then recounted the horror of losing them, although there was one detail she left out.

Baxter listened with a combination of compassion, interest, and horror to Faith's confession about her loss. He heard every nuance in her voice and sometimes bent forward to watch the myriad expressions animating her face. And, in doing so, he experienced her pain. When she finished and lay listless in his arms, he smoothed a hand down her tearstained cheek, and although there were no words, he tried anyway. "I'm so sorry, Faith. You've endured more than anyone should have to, but you've survived. You've come to Somewhere trying to go on with your life and I admire you for that. And I'm behind you a hundred percent." He paused because words were so inadequate. Finally, he said, "I care for you."

She shifted in his arms until she was gazing up at him, and in a voice broken with sorrow admitted, "I haven't spoken to anyone like this, not even my sister or friends. I pushed everyone away. They wanted me to see a counselor, but I just couldn't bring myself to unload my feelings. But now I-I somehow feel lighter. Like I've done the right thing. Thank you for listening."

Staring at Faith's mouth, Baxter wanted to kiss her grief away. He wanted to taste that sweetness that called to him like an angelic song. He wanted to lay her across his bed and return both of them to the innocence of first love. Was it possible? He doubted it. Instead, he bent and kissed her forehead.

24: Michael

Michael David Wainwright, III, pulled his car to the curb on Ocean Boulevard and studied the circular drive of the house he was interested in. He noted the information on the real estate sign and then made a U-turn and drove north along the boulevard to the public beach parking lot. He spotted an empty space and parked his Mercedes Cabriolet. Because he had driven directly from his office in Portland, he still wore his Brooks Brothers' suit and Hugo Boss shoes. Stepping outside the car he removed his shoes and socks and tossed them onto the floorboard of the back seat. He then engaged his security system before walking to the shore. Following it south, he enjoyed the squish of sand beneath his feet. The bottom of his slacks, although he'd rolled them up, became soaked, but he didn't care. He reached the private beach for Ocean Boulevard residents and ignored the signpost warning that it was closed to the public, continuing on. Glancing occasionally at his Baume and Mercier watch, he noted how far he'd walked. When it was the same distance he'd calculated after driving away from the house, he crossed the sand until he stood at a low, natural rock wall separating the houses from the beach. The home in front of him was the one for sale. Although not nearly as fantastic as some of his other homes, it was impressive and he loved the location. Of course, if he purchased the house he would have the latest security equipment installed so that even an ant crossing the boundary would set it off.

He saw some stairs traversing the rocky outcropping and climbed them to check out the house. After a short time he returned to his car and spoke to the infotaintment system. "Give me the number for McGovern Real Estate in Somewhere, Oregon."

The virtual operator found the number and asked, "Would you like me to dial that number?"

"Yes."

After two rings a young woman cheerily answered, "Good afternoon. McGovern Real Estate."

"Good afternoon. I'd like to speak with the agent handling the home at 1111 Ocean Boulevard."

"Yes, sir. That would be Dave or Doris McGovern. Please hold a moment."

The phone went to Kenny G playing Songbird but only lasted a few seconds before a woman answered. "Hello. This is Doris McGovern. How can I help you?"

"I'm interested in the home at 1111 Ocean Boulevard."

"I can certainly understand why. It's beautiful and very reasonably priced. Would you like to schedule a tour?"

Michael knew he was about to shock the agent when he said, "No. I'd like to buy it and I'll pay the asking price. I want to use my own title company and complete the purchase in less than two weeks."

The other end of the phone went silent as Michael waited for Mrs. McGovern to recover herself. When she did, to her credit, she said calmly, "Why don't I get some information so we can start the process?"

After giving Mrs. McGovern the information she needed and hanging up, Michael turned the ignition, grinned at the purr of the biturbo engine, and continued north on the boulevard. At another location, before reaching the intersection of Main Street, he pulled to the curb to scan a portion of the public beach full of beach goers. He grinned. *Yep, this is the perfect spot for my next resort.*

Leo answered his cell phone and tried to sound friendly. He had just disconnected from a call informing him that his wine order had been delayed yet again, and he was fuming. That particular brand was a house favorite and he was down to ten bottles.

"Leo, you okay? You sound angry.

This is Doris."

He puffed a breath. "Damn, but you're good. I was trying my best *not* to sound angry. How did you know?"

She laughed. "It comes from years of having to read people. And speaking of that..." her voice trailed.

"Yes?"

"Well, I just got a call from a guy who wants to buy the Jones place on Ocean Boulevard. And he's going to pay cash..." Her voice trailed again.

"And that's bad because..."

"The fact that he wants to pay cash isn't bad, but the fact that his name is Michael David Wainwright, III, is. I looked him up on the internet and he's–"

Leo finished her sentence. "–the CEO and major stockholder of Wainwright Resorts. Shit! Ah, sorry about the language, Doris."

"Do you think he wants to infiltrate Somewhere and build a resort?"

Leo didn't want to say too much. "Could be."

Doris was silent again and then said, "But we've had developers here before and the council always turns them away. You don't think the new members could be swayed after almost a century of councils upholding the wishes of the citizens of Somewhere."

Although Leo wanted to say, "Bingo," he instead said, "I sure hope not."

Doris sounded concerned. "What should I do? I can't legally keep this guy from buying the property."

"Can you stall him?"

"Maybe for a while, but if he found out it could put my license in jeopardy. Besides, he could just find another agent."

"That's true. It's better to know what he's up to than to wonder. Stall him if you can, but don't lose the sale. I'll see what I can find out and get back to you."

After he disconnected, Leo hung his head. He had a feeling his beloved Somewhere was in trouble. A few minutes later he called Gabby and insisted they talk. When she asked if it had anything to do with their last discussion his hesitation gave him away. She said, "Okay. Do you want to come over to the B & B?"

"I can't right now. I'm in the middle of a wine debacle. Why don't you come to the restaurant for lunch?"

Now Gabby hesitated. Finally, she said, "All right. I'll come over there."

"Perfect."

Gabby sat across from Leo in a darkened corner of his restaurant selected for privacy and listened to his latest news about a possible corporate infringement on their town. When he finished speaking she said, "That's terrible news. Why do you think the owner of the company would want to buy a home here?"

"Maybe to put pressure on council members?"

"Sounds reasonable."

Leo shrugged. "Or maybe he just loves

the ocean and wants a vacation home."

Gabby lifted her eyebrows.

His mouth quirked. "One can hope."

She decided to change the subject. "What's your wine debacle?"

He grinned. "Are you actually making conversation with me, Gabby?"

She frowned. "If you're going to be a smart ass, I can leave since you've delivered the bad news."

Leo reached and touched her arm. "I wasn't trying to be a smart ass. I was making a stupid joke. Don't leave." He then delved into the trouble he was having with his wine distributor and his own search for several cases of the merlot he wanted.

Later, after a delicious lunch of fruit salad, maple salmon over a bed of rice, rolls, mango tea, and rum panna cotta for dessert, Gabby glanced at her watch and was shocked to discover she and Leo had been talking for almost two hours. Breaking into his conversation she said, "I didn't realize it was so late. I've got to get back to the B & B. I have new arrivals expected this afternoon."

As she reached for her purse Leo said, "Maybe we can do this again?"

Gabby shifted her gaze to his and felt trapped by his eyes. She'd always thought them beautiful. He reached to touch her hand and said low, "It's still between us, Gabby. You can run, but it won't go away. Have dinner with me tomorrow. We'll go to Brookings to avoid prying eyes."

Gabby's voice cracked. "No. There's nothing between us and I won't have dinner with you."

The sadness in Leo's expressive eyes was almost her undoing and she quickly left the table.

25: Resolve

Faith sat on the edge of her bed staring at the painting of Owen and Rex. It had been two days since her meltdown with Baxter, and because of his kindness, she'd felt something shift within her. Somehow, her sorrow wasn't as debilitating, and she was actually contemplating a future in Somewhere.

She studied Owen's face and whispered, "What a sweet boy you must have been." As for her encounter with a child named Owen upon her arrival, she'd chalked it up to meeting a tourist's child who happened to resemble Owen, have the same name, and a similar dog. And the voice she'd heard twice at Stone House was something subliminal she'd overheard and carried over into her conscious mind, just as Baxter had suggested. The final hurdle though—the strange things Gabby had told her—well, they had to be more coincidences, because the alternative was impossible.

She reached for the painting to rewrap it. She would store it under her bed and go on with life. That was her resolve.

After supper Baxter called to her as she headed upstairs to spend the remainder of the evening writing her pirate story.

"Faith!"

She turned and admonished her stomach to stop doing summersaults, but instead, it did back flips at the smile he gave her.

"Come walk with me on the beach."

She bit her bottom lip and then realized he might get the impression that she was trying to find a way to say no. "All right. Give me a minute to change my shoes."

"Great. I'll meet you on the front porch."

Two minutes later she was hurrying back downstairs and outside. Baxter was talking to his mother and when he saw her, his face lit with another smile. She glanced at Gabby to see that she, too, was grinning like a Cheshire cat. Gabby said, "You kids have fun."

As Baxter held Faith's elbow and guided her down the porch steps to the sidewalk, he chuckled. "I think I'll be a perpetual kid to my mother, even when I'm fifty."

Faith replied, "You better get used to it. That's how mothers are." When they reached the crosswalk that would take them to the B & B's private beach, Baxter didn't step onto it. Instead, he bent his knees until he was Faith's height. "How are you doing?"

Faith had the notion he was asking because of her comment about mothers. If she'd said something like that a few days ago, it would have been heartrending, but now it was just a remark. She almost reached to cup his cheek. "I'm doing very well and that's the honest truth."

He reached for her hand. "Good. Now let's play tag with the waves." He playfully pulled her across the street and onto the sand. They paused long enough to remove their flip flops and then jogged to the water, splashing up to their knees. Later they walked to the tree line and Baxter asked if she wanted to follow the trail into the woods, but she declined by saying, "I'm having too much fun on the beach."

He grinned and grabbed her hand. "I am too." They ran back to the shore and he splashed her. She sputtered and called out, "You'll be sorry."

For maybe an hour they cavorted until Faith sat in the sand exhausted and Baxter sat beside her. He smirked, "I'm still waiting to be sorry."

She laughed and met his gaze and was about to make a snarky reply, but his expression held such intensity that she couldn't breathe, and when his gaze dropped to her mouth, she felt like he was touching her. He bent and grazed his lips across her forehead. Speaking softly, he said, "I want to kiss you. May I?"

Tears flooded Faith's eyes.

He moved his mouth to her ear. "I want to kiss your tears away."

Slowly, Faith nodded and closed her eyes. She felt the gentle touch of his lips on hers and marveled at her response. She *wanted* him to kiss her, hold her, touch her, and she wanted to do the same to him. His mouth moved over hers and she whimpered. He deepened the kiss, but not much. She reached to touch his shoulder and became braver, lifting her arms around his neck. After that the sound of the ocean, laughter of beach goers, cars in the distance, everything faded into nothingness. She and Baxter were the only people on earth.

Gabby stood at the third floor window in her sitting room and watched her son and Faith lying in the sand kissing. A tiny smile lifted the corners of her mouth. Maybe Baxter and Faith could heal each other's sorrow. Maybe someday she would have grandchildren.

She closed her eyes and remembered

another kiss that shouldn't have happened, and although it had been decades earlier, in her mind it was as fresh as the day it transpired—and so was her guilt. At that time she had just married a wonderful man that she adored. Was it possible to love two men at the same time? She opened her eyes and a tear trickled. Her luncheon with Leo had been wonderful and she wondered for a moment what her life would have been like had she met Leo before Marcus. Even now, however, she knew she would have made the same decision. Marcus was a man of stability, and since Gabby had been raised by hippies, she needed constancy. And Leo, a young, handsome surfer, was exactly what she didn't need or want.

But what did she want now? Although vestiges of her hippie years remained, she was an upstanding business woman with an orderly life, and well respected in Somewhere. She'd had a wonderful marriage that produced a son she adored. What more could she ask for?

Her wayward mind refused to be silenced. *How about a man who adores you and makes your heart race? A man who loves adventure and still surfs. A man devoted to you. A man...*

She shut her thoughts down with just one thought: *You're too old for this.*

26: Commission

Michael said goodbye to Doris McGovern and disconnected his cell phone. He was well aware that she was trying to postpone his purchase of the beach house. Of course, he could contact another realtor to finish his acquisition, but he liked the McGoverns.

No doubt she had researched him on the internet and connected the dots. She may have even made inquiries of someone with inside knowledge of his private meeting with council members. He chuckled because he knew how small town politics worked. Over the years, he'd been through the process many times trying to get approval for his resorts.

He stepped away from his desk and walked to the expansive windows overlooking the Willamette River. He'd known that constructing a resort in Somewhere would involve an abundance of headaches, and that another location along the coast could easily be

negotiated, but there was something about Somewhere that touched his heart.

He turned from the windows and scanned his spacious office. His company leased the entire top floor of a mid-rise in the Pearl District of Portland, and although he'd considered buying his own building, one of the reasons he was at the top of the food chain was because of wise investments, calculated spending, and low overhead in comparison to the magnitude of his company.

He had been born with a silver spoon in his mouth, but his father had been foolish with the management of the company inherited after his own father's untimely death. By the time Michael had taken over the reins the business had been well on its way to insolvency. And although his lifestyle had been luxurious growing up, he'd often wondered when his family would become tabloid fodder as he watched his father's business ventures and personal life become irrational.

And then it happened. His father put his family and business forever on the "scandalous" map when he'd met his demise at the age of fifty-two in a car accident with two hookers. The hookers survived and sold their stories to sleazy newspapers, which ended his mother's social status, and she'd committed suicide a year later.

In a nutshell, his home life had been absurdly dysfunctional, which was one of the reasons he'd never married. Now, sixteen years later, after assuming the reins of the family business at the age of twenty-three, his company was successful and he was fabulously rich. He had much to be proud of, but as of late, it seemed to matter less and less.

Making a spur-of-the-moment decision he strode across the room and opened his door. "Leticia, how many appointments do I have this afternoon?"

"Two, sir."

"Can they be cancelled?"

His secretary knew the company as

well as he did and replied without looking at his schedule, "They sure can. Are you taking the rest of the day off?"

"I'm thinking about it."

"Well, I say go for it. George can handle any emergencies."

Michael smiled at the sixty-one year old, gray haired secretary that had been with him for fifteen years and sometimes acted like the mother he should have had. "I'm outta here."

"Where are you going?"

"Somewhere."

Michael enjoyed the three hour drive to the coastal town and arrived a little after three. He drove through downtown and turned onto Ocean Boulevard. After passing the public beach he admired the homes, especially his, as he headed toward the marina. He felt excitement over knowing he would soon join the neighborhood. When he reached the marina, he scanned the many vessels, from sailboats to fishing craft, to dinghies, to small yachts, and decided it was a nice enough marina for docking his smallest yacht. He reentered the boulevard and even considered dining at Seafood Heaven, but decided against it. For now it was best to remain incognito.

Returning to Main Street he saw a sign that caught his attention, Art's Art Gallery, and weighed his desire to stay anonymous with his love of the arts. Art won.

He parked down the street from the gallery and walked back, loving the sun and breeze on such a fine day. Before leaving Portland he'd shed his business suit in favor of tacky jeans, an old T-shirt, and his favorite worn-out tennis shoes. He looked like a beach bum.

Michael entered the gallery and a bell tinkled. A clerk stepped from the backroom, perused his appearance, and seemed disinclined to engage him in conversation. With a bored expression the man said, "Welcome to my gallery. I'm Art and I feature mostly local artists. Are you looking for anything in

214

particular?"

Michael was an excellent judge of character and knew he was getting the spiel for unimpressive tourists. He replied with the usual comment, "No. I'm just browsing."

When the proprietor appeared utterly uninterested in even making polite conversation about the weather, Michael inwardly fumed. His resorts were successful because he catered to customers, and, without a doubt, he would fire any employee who treated a customer like Art had just treated him.

The man waved toward his desk at the back of the room. "I'll be at my desk if you have questions."

The only reason Michael didn't leave was because he was interested in local artists. He always displayed their artwork at his resorts. In fact, several artisans had become well known after their pieces were discovered in his world-class accommodations.

He wandered the room perusing the

artwork and picking up business cards until he'd accumulated maybe six or seven. He would research the artists online. When he came to an alcove, he was more than impressed by the paintings displayed there. The artist had created wonderful scenes of the past juxtaposed to the present within the same paintings. One scene was that of Main Street with half the street being current day and the other, early 20th century. Some of the paintings were whimsical, others dark and mysterious. He particularly liked the one of Hope Bed & Breakfast with modern day tourists on the porch and sidewalk, contrasted with its beach full of Victorian beachgoers. He stepped out of the alcove and called, "Art, what can you tell me about these paintings signed by Vee?" He heard the man's chair scrape the floor and imagined the rude curator being irritated by an interruption.

With a phony smile, Art walked to the alcove. "They were painted by Victoria

Patterson who runs the Museum."

"She's very good."

"Yes. But she said she wasn't going to paint anything else for a while because she's trying her hand at sculpting. Maybe it isn't going so well. So far she hasn't brought any sculptures in." He motioned toward the paintings. "I tried to get her to lower the prices on these, but she refused."

Michael fumed again. The impolite man was offering up negative information on the artist and disagreeing publicly with her price point. "Wise woman," he retorted. "Wrap them all up; I want them." He heard the curator gasp and turned to stare at him. Cryptically, he said, "Book. Cover. Think about it."

By the time Michael left the gallery, Art was doing everything but somersaults to ingratiate himself with his latest customer. He even gave him a hundred dollar gift certificate toward his next purchase. Other than his veiled rebuke spoken earlier, Michael was polite and friendly. After all, he would soon become one of the locals.

He loaded the five paintings into the trunk of his car, climbed behind the wheel, and made a U-turn at the first stoplight. He was headed toward the sign he'd seen earlier indicating that Hope Museum was down a side street. As it turned out, it wasn't far off Main and he pulled into the parking lot on the side of the manor. The Victorian home was lovely and the grounds well manicured. The exterior paint wasn't flaking or the porch sagging. Everything, he noted, was geared toward the era of the home, even the WELCOME and HOURS signs were period appropriate. He entered the front door and was greeted by a woman sitting behind a spinet desk. She appeared to be drawing something, but placed a newspaper over the page. She was dressed in a Victorian gown the same color as her emerald eyes and said cheerily, "Good afternoon and welcome to Hope Museum. We close at five, but if you need more time, I can give you a pass for another day and a tour."

Michael replied, "Thank you. But right now I'm looking for Victoria Patterson." When the lady's face showed surprise, he knew he was talking to her.

"I'm Victoria."

He smiled. "My name is Michael and I just bought all your paintings from Art's Art Gallery." He purposely did not reveal his last name.

Her expressive eyes widened and she seemed at a loss for words. Finally, she blurted, "Thank you!"

Michael decided to get to the crux of his visit. "I drove down from Portland for the day and happened upon your paintings. I'm very impressed by your talent. Is there somewhere we can talk?"

Again, the woman seemed flummoxed, but motioned down the hall. "There's a parlor that's also a souvenir shop this way."

He followed her and admired the care given to the interior of the home. The museum was obviously special to someone, and he suspected it was Victoria. When she motioned for him to sit on a settee, he said, "After you, ma'am." She sat on the edge of the red velvet cushion and he took up an easy posture at the other end. He commented on the red velvet draperies and a few artifacts in the room before getting to the reason for his visit. "The reason I'm here is because I want to commission you to paint several local scenes in the same vein as the ones I purchased." He noted her surprise before adding, "And I'll pay you very well. If you decide to accept the commission, we can work out an amount that is suitable to your talent." She seemed to be at a loss for words.

Finally, she said, "I'm not a well known artist, even in town. There are artisans living here much more talented than I."

Michael liked her humility. "I beg to differ. Of all the paintings in the gallery, yours appealed to me the most. I've just purchased a new home and since I'm

well connected to connoisseurs of the art world, yours will be seen by them." He purposely allowed her to believe the paintings were for his home. If allowed to build the resort, he would surprise her with the knowledge that they would hang there, if denied; the paintings *would* hang in his home.

She twisted her hands in her lap. "I'm not looking to break into the art world. It's just a hobby I enjoy."

Michael studied the green depth of her eyes and instinctively knew she was a woman of many layers. He also noted that in no way had she attempted to flirt with him, which was refreshing. He was often the target of women who admired his looks, but when wealth was added, he became irresistible to them. This woman appeared to care nothing about his outward appearance or his money, even though she must have intuited from their conversation that he was affluent.

He stood to leave. "Just think about it, and when I'm back in town I'll stop by for

that tour and your answer." He could see relief in her eyes that he wasn't pressing her for a response.

"I'll do that."

Vicky watched the door close behind the stunningly handsome man and breathed a sigh of relief. The entire time they had talked she had wanted to stare continuously at such male perfection. Whenever she'd met his gaze she had almost drowned in their depths. Never had she seen eyes the color of honey. She decided his name of Michael suited him well. *He looks like a fallen angel.* She sat at her desk, leaned her elbow on the antique surface, and placed her chin in her palm. *He purchased all my paintings! And he wants to commission more!* This would require some serious consideration on her part.

Later, after she'd closed the museum and retired to the third floor, she sat before the window in her sitting room and stared at the waning sun. For the

well connected to connoisseurs of the art world, yours will be seen by them." He purposely allowed her to believe the paintings were for his home. If allowed to build the resort, he would surprise her with the knowledge that they would hang there, if denied; the paintings *would* hang in his home.

She twisted her hands in her lap. "I'm not looking to break into the art world. It's just a hobby I enjoy."

Michael studied the green depth of her eyes and instinctively knew she was a woman of many layers. He also noted that in no way had she attempted to flirt with him, which was refreshing. He was often the target of women who admired his looks, but when wealth was added, he became irresistible to them. This woman appeared to care nothing about his outward appearance or his money, even though she must have intuited from their conversation that he was affluent.

He stood to leave. "Just think about it, and when I'm back in town I'll stop by for

that tour and your answer." He could see relief in her eyes that he wasn't pressing her for a response.

"I'll do that."

Vicky watched the door close behind the stunningly handsome man and breathed a sigh of relief. The entire time they had talked she had wanted to stare continuously at such male perfection. Whenever she'd met his gaze she had almost drowned in their depths. Never had she seen eyes the color of honey. She decided his name of Michael suited him well. *He looks like a fallen angel.* She sat at her desk, leaned her elbow on the antique surface, and placed her chin in her palm. *He purchased all my paintings! And he wants to commission more!* This would require some serious consideration on her part.

Later, after she'd closed the museum and retired to the third floor, she sat before the window in her sitting room and stared at the waning sun. For the

well connected to connoisseurs of the art world, yours will be seen by them." He purposely allowed her to believe the paintings were for his home. If allowed to build the resort, he would surprise her with the knowledge that they would hang there, if denied; the paintings *would* hang in his home.

She twisted her hands in her lap. "I'm not looking to break into the art world. It's just a hobby I enjoy."

Michael studied the green depth of her eyes and instinctively knew she was a woman of many layers. He also noted that in no way had she attempted to flirt with him, which was refreshing. He was often the target of women who admired his looks, but when wealth was added, he became irresistible to them. This woman appeared to care nothing about his outward appearance or his money, even though she must have intuited from their conversation that he was affluent.

He stood to leave. "Just think about it, and when I'm back in town I'll stop by for

that tour and your answer." He could see relief in her eyes that he wasn't pressing her for a response.

"I'll do that."

Vicky watched the door close behind the stunningly handsome man and breathed a sigh of relief. The entire time they had talked she had wanted to stare continuously at such male perfection. Whenever she'd met his gaze she had almost drowned in their depths. Never had she seen eyes the color of honey. She decided his name of Michael suited him well. *He looks like a fallen angel.* She sat at her desk, leaned her elbow on the antique surface, and placed her chin in her palm. *He purchased all my paintings! And he wants to commission more!* This would require some serious consideration on her part.

Later, after she'd closed the museum and retired to the third floor, she sat before the window in her sitting room and stared at the waning sun. For the

millionth time she wished the window were large enough to afford a view of the ocean. She closed her eyes to relive Michael's visit and wondered what his last name was. *What a classy man.*

After a time she sighed, stood, and thought about what to prepare for dinner. As she turned, she caught sight of the envelope with a check for her painting of Owen and Rex that had sold at the street festival. She'd been shocked and her first question to Art was, "Who bought it?" His reply had been curt, "Some tourist."

Now, staring at the envelope, she was tempted to toss it in the trash. Somehow it seemed wrong to make money from a painting of her twin brother whose death haunted her to this day. Because of his death, her father had deserted his family and her mother had lost contact with reality. Even now, Ann Patterson lived in an institution. Most days she could function fairly well, but other days she became depressed and suicidal. *And all because of me.*

27: Dilemma

Faith laughed when Baxter pulled her into a closet on the second floor landing, closed the door, and said in her ear, "Just one kiss, lovely lady, and I promise to leave you alone for at least an hour."

She turned her face into his neck and mumbled, "And if I refuse?"

He said low, "Are you going to refuse?"

"No."

"Then I have my answer, fair maiden."

Before she could respond with her own quip, he was kissing her with such passion that she forgot what she was about to say. And the fact that one kiss turned into many, didn't bother her in the least. When he broke away and leaned his head against hers, his breathing was rapid. "I'm crazy about you, Faith."

She nuzzled against his chest. "Bax, you make me feel alive again."

He chuckled and moved his hands from her back to encircle her waist. "You do know, don't you, that you're the only one allowed to call me Bax."

"Would you rather I didn't?"

"Hell, no." And with those words he started kissing her again.

There was a rap on the door. "Baxter, I need your help in the garden. And Faith, I just placed a basket of fresh bread on the table."

Baxter mumbled a curse and Faith giggled. "I swear your mother is psychic. Either that or she has hidden cameras in every room."

Baxter gave her a quick kiss. "As soon as I help my mother and answer my emails, I'll meet you on the beach, probably between three and three-thirty."

Faith arrived at the B & B's private beach at two-thirty, but walked along the shore until she reached the public beach. She and Baxter had decided to keep their relationship private to avoid questions from guests. She set her umbrella up and then spread her towel on the sand. For two weeks she and Baxter had been flirting and kissing, but most of all *talking.* He had confided in her about his marriage and divorce and she had opened up about her husband and child. At times, their confidences were emotional and difficult, but throughout it all, they realized they were healing and coming to a place where they could go on with their lives.

Faith sat on her towel, gazed at lapping waves, and smiled. Baxter was a wonderful man and she was falling for him, but where that would lead, she didn't know. For now, however, her ability to move beyond her sorrow was enough.

After a time, the warmth of the sun and the backdrop hum of waves and laughter caused her to drift into the realm between awareness and sleep. She felt languid and happy.

"Rex!"

At first, recognition of the name played tag with her semiconscious mind, but when she heard it again, she jerked upright.

She heard it a third time. "Rex!"

Scanning the beach to the south she squinted into the haze and then moved her gaze past a man and woman walking hand-in-hand beside the water's edge. Beyond them a game of volleyball was being played by several teenagers. Then she saw a boy in the distance. He was wearing a blue ball cap and tossing a Frisbee for a big, red dog.

Faith jumped to her feet and started running toward them. She passed the couple who had turned around and were now walking toward her. They smiled, but she didn't acknowledge them. Then she weaved around the volleyball game. A few more tourists remained between her and the boy, but finally she was close enough to realize it was the child from her first encounter. She called, "Owen!"

He turned at the sound of his name and smiled. Then he tossed the Frisbee for Rex farther down the beach. The dog barked happily and ran after it. Owen ran after his dog.

She called again, "Wait for me!"

The boy looked back and shouted, "Tell Vee it wasn't her fault!" He started running after the dog.

Heedless of her surroundings, Faith chased them, but suddenly found herself toppled to the ground when her feet got tangled up in someone's towel. She heard a man say, "Lady, are you okay?" She ignored the question. She had to reach Owen. She pushed upward and searched for the boy. There was no boy and no dog. She jerked her head in every direction, but only saw tourists. The man repeated, "Are you okay? You seem disoriented."

She glanced up at a short, middle-aged guy with a large girth. "Did you just see a boy in a blue ball cap tossing a Frisbee for a large red dog?" She pointed. "Over there."

"Ah, no. But then I wasn't paying attention to anyone over there."

She jumped to her feet and ran in the

direction she had indicated. When she reached the location where Owen and Rex had been, she searched for footprints, even as waves lapped the sand. She thought she saw a paw print and rushed toward it. A wave covered it, and when it receded, the print was gone.

Tears stung Faith's eyes. Was she losing her mind?

By the time she returned to her umbrella and towel, Baxter was striding toward her wearing his bathing trunks and carrying a large picnic basket. She considered telling him about what had just happened, but immediately discarded that notion. He would either think she was crazy or trying to trick him into something. When he reached her, he asked, "What's wrong?"

"I-I'm not feeling well. I think I should return to my room and rest."

"Do you need to see a doctor?"

"No. It's nothing as severe as that. I'm just feeling a little queasy."

Hastily, Baxter closed Faith's umbrella

and tossed her towel on top of the picnic basket. Holding her elbow, he walked her back to the B & B, and when they entered the house he discarded the items he was carrying and placed his arm around her. "I'll help you to your room, honey."

His endearment and kindness touched Faith's heart and she wanted to turn into his arms and cry. Instead, she merely mumbled her assent and allowed him to guide her upstairs. In her room, she lay across her bed and covered her eyes with her forearm.

Baxter sounded worried when he said, "Maybe we should call the doctor just in case."

"No, please just give me an hour and then see how I feel."

He hesitated but finally agreed. "Okay. One hour. Would you like my mother to help you change out of your bathing suit?"

"No. I can do it."

Again Baxter hesitated. "Can I bring you some tea?"

"No. I just want to rest." She felt the gentle brush of his lips on the top of her head.

"Okay, but I'll be back periodically to check on you."

"Thank you, Baxter."

It wasn't long after Baxter left that there was a soft knock on her door and it opened before she could respond. Gabby stuck her head around the corner. "Baxter said you're ill. Can I come in?"

Faith stifled a sob. "Yes. I really need to talk to you." Gabby frowned as she entered the room and hurried to the bedside. Gently sitting on the edge of it, she said, "Hon, this is more than illness. What happened?"

This time Faith couldn't hold back a sob. "I talked to Owen again!"

Back in her suite, Gabby splashed water on her face and stared at her reflection in the bathroom mirror. The tale Faith had just shared still made the hair on her arms stand up. Had she really spoken to a boy who had been dead for over twenty years? Or was she so engulfed in her own sorrow that somehow conjuring up this child helped her? If not for the psychic's words from three years earlier and the story about Mr. Lucky, she'd tend to go with the latter explanation, but now she was starting to believe in ghosts. She picked up a brush and began combing her long locks.

Faith had begged her not to say anything to Baxter and she could understand why. Her son would surely think he was being played for a fool and break off their budding romance. And that was the last thing Gabby wanted. Her boy was finally becoming human again and not the automaton he'd turned into.

So what should Faith do with the message from Owen? And what should she, herself, do about the message from the psychic? Both of them were faced with a dilemma.

28: Key

Michael signed the last document set before him and grinned. He now owned the home on Ocean Boulevard and perhaps in the future he would own a resort on that same road. He handed the pen back to the escrow officer and reached to shake Doris McGovern's hand, and then her husband's. Neither of them appeared happy about the transaction, even though it would yield them an outstanding commission. To their credit, they'd kept the sale in limbo, but finally, after a not so subtle innuendo that another real estate agent had offered to assist in the sale, they'd stepped up to the plate.

Tossing the house key in his hand, Michael walked to his car. He felt like celebrating. Even if he failed to get approval for his resort, he'd have gone ahead with the purchase anyway. He loved the friendliness of the community and the beauty of the cove. He'd even assigned his P.I. to start an investigation of the town and its occupants. Of course, before initially deciding to bring his resort to Somewhere, he'd done his own research and knew that Gabby Hope owned the northern peninsula, while Leo Constanzo owned the southern. However, his investigator had recently discovered there was bad blood between them, although the reason was unknown. Michael had instructed the P.I. to keep searching. He'd also asked for research on Victoria Patterson, the museum curator. She fascinated him. She wasn't beautiful or even striking as far as her outward appearance, but something exceptional radiated from within that he couldn't put his finger on. And an hour before signing his loan docs his investigator had called and given a report on her. Michael was surprised to learn that she was a twin and at the age of nine her brother and his dog had drowned. No one had witnessed the drowning and the bodies had washed ashore on the beach of the northern peninsula a day after going missing. The death of the boy had devastated the family and his mother had started consulting psychics. The father had eventually left and the mother was now institutionalized.

Turning the ignition of his Porsche, Michael released a long sigh. His own life had been visited with sorrow, so maybe that's why he was drawn to Vicky. He pulled away from the curb and at the intersection turned his vehicle in the direction of the museum.

Vicky was dusting the mantle in the library when she heard the bell over the door sound. Quickly she stashed the dust rag in a corner of a bookshelf and went to greet her guest. Her heart slammed her chest when she recognized the gentleman from three weeks previous. He grinned and said, "Hello again. My schedule is clear so I'm ready for that tour."

Vicky pushed a wayward strand of

black hair behind her ear and smoothed a hand down her dress. At least two days a week she always dressed Victorian and today she wore a burgundy silk day dress with rounded neckline, sloping shoulders, pagoda sleeves, and a triple flounced green underskirt. It was one of her favorites.

Before she could respond the man stuck out his hand. "Hi, Vicky. Michael again."

"Ah, yes, yes. I remember you." She felt flustered and embarrassed by her girlish reaction and tried to sound professional when she continued, "Before the tour, let me get you a brochure that describes the rooms in the house." She reached toward her desk, but accidentally bumped the vase of flowers she'd picked and arranged that morning. She gasped and lunged to prevent a spill at the same time as Michael, and they collided. With one hand he grasped the vase and with the other he clasped her upper arm. She stared up into his honey colored eyes.

Neither of them moved for a second and then she jumped back. Mortified, she exclaimed, "I am *so* sorry!" She could feel her face flaming scarlet.

Her guest seemed unperturbed. "Accidents happen." He reached to move the vase away from the edge of the desk.

Still reeling by her contact with Michael, Vicky glanced at her watch, thankful for the distraction. "My assistant should arrive in fifteen minutes. I can't leave my post until then."

"Not a problem. I have some phone calls to make, so I'll see you in fifteen." He gave her a disarming grin and then retreated out the front door.

Vicky sank onto the chair behind her desk and stared at the vase of gladiolas. She was a complete dork when it came to men.

Ten minutes later her assistant arrived and five minutes after that Michael reentered the museum. Vicky watched her young helper's eyes widen at the sight of such a handsome man. "Sarah,

I'm taking this gentleman on a tour of the museum so you're in charge. But just so you know, a sixth grade school group is expected to arrive around ten-thirty. I should be back by then, if not, text me."

"Yes, ma'am," said the sixteen year old and grinned coyly at Michael.

Inwardly, Vicky sighed.

29: Flood

Gabby entered Seafood Heaven and waited for the hostess to return to her station. Leo had called and said they needed to talk, but that he couldn't get away from the restaurant. She wondered if he was setting her up for another luncheon with him. Noah walked past the station and saw her. "Hi, Aunt Gabby. Gramps told me you were coming over."

"He said he needed to talk but couldn't get away."

"That's for sure. He discovered a cracked pipe in the basement this morning and the plumber left about an hour ago. Gramps has been cleaning up the mess."

"Is he still in the basement?"

"Probably. Come on back to the kitchen."

She followed her nephew to the swinging doors and as soon as they entered the chef said, "Noah, table four is ready."

Noah said to Gabby, "We just got back to serving and we're down a waiter. Can you find your way to the basement?"

"I think I still know the way." She motioned toward a second door and Noah nodded. "Follow the hallway to the back."

The chef said, "Noah, the food is getting cold."

As Noah rushed to the warming shelf he called, "I'll catch you later, Aunt Gabby."

"Sure thing, Noah." Although she had a passing acquaintance with the chef and some of the employees, they were all too busy to give her more than a nod. Following the hallway past several doors, she came to the end and lightly knocked. There was no answer so she opened it and called, "Leonardo, are you down there?"

There was a shuffling and then, "Yes, *Gabriella.* Come on down."

By the way he'd emphasized her name, she knew he wasn't happy about being called Leonardo, but she didn't care. She descended the stairs and saw him pushing a shop-vac toward a puddle of water. He glanced up. "This is the last of the disaster. Just give me a few minutes."

Gabby nodded and sat on a stair halfway down. In a short time the puddle was sucked dry and Leo was pushing the vacuum to a corner. When he started up the stairs, she rose, but he made a downward motion. "Stay there. I need to rest a minute. I've been cleaning for over an hour." He sat beside her, forcing her to scoot over. She wanted to move to another stair, but that would only let him know how much he affected her. He released a long sigh. "I'm getting too old for catastrophes like this."

Gabby didn't want to make small talk so she said pointedly, "Why did you ask me here. Is it about Wainwright?"

Leo chuckled. "I love it when you put me in my place. And yes, it's about the resort. Dave McGovern called and said

Mr. Wainwright signed the papers for the Ocean Boulevard house. Now the guy has a home in our town and I fully expect he'll begin courting the town council."

Gabby placed her elbows on her knees and her chin in her hands. "Rats."

Leo murmured something in agreement and then became silent. Finally, he said, "You might as well eat lunch with me since you're here."

Gabby frowned. "I've got too much happening at the B & B." She started to rise, but Leo touched her arm. Being so close, as soon as her eyes met his, she knew she was in trouble.

He said softly, "You came here because you wanted to see me. You could have insisted I tell you my news over the phone."

She couldn't remove her gaze from his, and it was only when his lips touched hers that she closed her eyes. Magically, the years faded and she was again that young woman being kissed by a man who made her heart both soar and hurt at the same time. He moved one hand to the back of her head and deepened the kiss. She gripped his shoulders, moving her mouth in synch with his. When he trailed his lips to her ear and said, "Gabby, I love you," she didn't push away. It was only when she felt tears welling that she pulled back, and, in direct opposition to what she really wanted, whispered, "No," then forcefully, "No!" She pushed at Leo's chest and he leaned back as a tear dripped down her cheek. "No, Leo. This is wrong."

He released her.

Face-to-face, he smiled sadly. "Gabby, for being such an intelligent woman, you're ruining what could become the happiest years of our lives."

"Marcus gave me the happiest years of my life."

His stare did not waver. "I'll not argue over words. You know what I meant. We could be very happy together."

Gabby stood and started backing up the stairs, then turned and rushed up them. When she entered the hallway she blinked back a flood of tears. At the kitchen door she paused to compose herself and then hurried through the room and into the dining area. Noah had his back to her conversing with patrons and she ignored the hostess' farewell as she escaped into the sunshine.

She cried all the way home.

30: Painting

Baxter had reached the breaking point. For five days Faith had been reclusive and inordinately quiet. At first he'd thought she was coming down with something, but after three days he'd suspected that wasn't the case. For the next two days he'd given her space, thinking she was having second thoughts about their burgeoning romance. But now he needed clarity. He needed to know what her feelings for him were, because he was crazy about her.

He knocked on her door once, twice, and when she cracked it open, they stared at each other. He was the first to speak. "May I come in?"

"I was just about to take a nap."

"This will only take a moment." When she didn't respond immediately he said, "Please, Faith. I have to talk to you."

She barely nodded and opened the door, and then walked to the window, waiting for him to speak.

He closed the door and said, "Faith, honey, something's going on that I don't understand. Talk to me."

She broke eye contact.

He said softly, "Are you having second thoughts about us?"

She nodded and his heart wrenched.

Unexpectedly, she said, "It has nothing to do with you though, and everything to do with me."

Inhaling, he replied, "What does that mean? Help me to understand."

She returned her gaze to his. "I have unresolved issues that you wouldn't understand."

When she didn't continue he prompted, "I want to understand because I care deeply for you. We've shared so much with each other that there's no reason to stop now. Talk to me, honey." He inhaled again and finally admitted, "I want our relationship to become more than a summer fling."

He watched an incredibly sad expression enter her eyes. "I can't go in that direction right now. I have to make sense of something first. Please don't pressure me because...because I care for you, too."

Baxter recognized the pleading in her eyes and acquiesced. "All right, Faith, if that's what you want." He swallowed the lump in his throat and turned to leave, but his gaze was drawn to something barely visible under the bed. He saw the artist's signature. "Is that one of Vicky's paintings?" He inclined his head toward the picture and heard Faith gasp.

When he walked over and reached to retrieve it, she exclaimed, "No! Don't!"

From his bent over position he glanced up at her stricken expression. Had he finally reached the crux of her "issue"? He ignored her request and pulled the partially wrapped picture from under the bed. His eyes widened when he saw Owen and Rex. Straightening and laying the painting on the quilt, he turned and said, "Why do you have this? Did you purchase it from the gallery?"

Faith's mouth opened but no words came out.

"Answer me, Faith."

She nodded.

"Of course my next question is why." He waited, and when she didn't answer, he sat on the edge of the bed next to the painting. He was determined to stay for as long as it took.

In a soft response she said, "I *did* see Owen and talk to him, but I convinced myself it wasn't really him, just a boy like him. When it happened again I knew it was him and Rex." With eyes luminous with tears she stared at Baxter.

He processed her admission. "You talked to him a second time?"

"Yes, the day you met me at the beach and I told you I was getting sick."

Slowly, Baxter stood. "And that's what's kept you so upset?"

She nodded.

He clenched his hands. "This game has gone on long enough. My emotions have been in turmoil worrying about you,

248

and now I find out you're still insisting that you talked to a *dead* boy." He started toward the door and when she said, "Baxter, I *did* talk to him," he shook his head in disbelief.

For a long time after Baxter left, Faith gazed out the window at the beach and contemplated her life. Of one thing she was sure, she could not continue living at the B & B. She sighed and closed her eyes. What were her alternatives: return to St. Louis, find another town, become a vagabond? No. She couldn't do any of the above. After several minutes reflection she retrieved her cell phone and called Doris McGovern.

"Hello, Faith. How are things going? I haven't spoken to you for a while. Are you still thinking of making Somewhere your home?"

"I am. In fact, I want to purchase the cottage on Haven Drive if it's still available."

Doris sounded surprised when she

responded, "Why yes, it's still on the market. Good for you. How would you like to proceed and when would you like to make a deposit?"

For several minutes the women discussed the purchasing process and when Faith disconnected the call, she said into the room, "Either I'm crazy, or something unfathomable has happened."

To avoid another encounter with Baxter, Faith ate dinner in her room and then telephoned Gabby, asking her to stop by. Within minutes Gabby knocked on her door and after both women were seated at the small oak table, Faith said, "Baxter came to see me today and it didn't turn out well."

Gabby leaned forward. "Was he terrible to you?"

"No, just honest. He expressed how much he cared for me and wanted to know what was wrong, but when he saw this…" She stood, walked to her bed, and reached under it for the painting. "It changed everything. I told him I'd had a second encounter with Owen and Rex and he didn't believe me."

"I'll talk to him," Gabby interjected.

"I don't want you to talk to him. That's not why I asked you here. I wanted to let you know that I'm leaving the B & B in three or four weeks."

"Oh, no. Are you returning to St. Louis?"

"No. I purchased the cottage on Haven Drive that I told you about."

Gabby's expression changed from one of concern to surprise, and then she smiled. "I'm so happy to hear that. Baxter will come around. I just know it."

"That's not the reason I'm staying in Somewhere. I had a moment of insight this afternoon that I can't explain. It brought clarity and I knew in my heart that I'm supposed to live here, but at the same time, I realized my decision to leave or stay couldn't be based on Baxter; it had to be based on me and something else." She hesitated before adding, "Discovering the reason for my bizarre encounters with Owen."

31: Revelation

Faith sat on the patio of her new home and listened to the bark of Dog and the laughter of Darren and Dirk in the yard behind her. As they did almost every day, the brothers were playing in their backyard, and, surprisingly, she looked forward to watching their antics. Her heart still hurt because of the loss of her own child, but somehow it had lessened since her arrival in Somewhere.

She gazed beyond the houses to the sea and then the peninsula owned by Gabby. Shifting her gaze to Ocean Boulevard, she followed the thoroughfare until she spotted what she thought was the magnificent home Doris and Dave had shown her, and wondered about the new owner. During the move to her cottage she had overheard gossip at Mama Pink's Diner that a wealthy business man had purchased the place and that his name was Michael Wainwright.

At the mention of his name, Vicky, who was dining with Faith at the time, gasped and almost spilled her tea. Curious, Faith responded by leaning forward and whispering, "Do you know him?"

"He's been to the museum a few times and I only recently discovered his last name. I know he's a successful business man who lives in Portland and he just bought a home, but I don't remember him telling me it was here."

She'd tapped her short, but pretty nails on the table and Faith knew she had more to say. Finally, she'd admitted, "He commissioned me to paint four pictures for him."

"That's wonderful!"

Without enthusiasm Vicky's response had been, "I was going to refuse, but after I got a letter from the government and discovered my portion of the monthly expense for my mother's care was going up, I decided to accept." She'd confided, "He's paying me a fortune."

"Are the pictures for his home?"

"That's what I assumed."

Returning her thoughts to the present, Faith moved her gaze farther down the boulevard and settled it on the marina owned by Leo. Mentally, she congratulated him on his well organized and successful marina, restaurant, and museum. A continuing curiosity, however, was Gabby's resistance to him. On the few occasions Faith had brought his name into their conversations, Gabby had either interjected a new topic or suddenly discovered she had errands to run. Faith knew the cousins-by-marriage had a longstanding rift, but she found it difficult to believe the bad feelings were a continuation of disagreements begun by their spouses' ancestors almost a century ago.

She surveyed the peninsula owned by Leo and then moved her gaze all the way back to Hope Bed & Breakfast and thought about Baxter. As expected, they avoided each other like the plague, but when they accidently met up, they were cordial. Vicky had once asked if the debacle about her brother had reared its head again and Faith's response had been, "We have different perspectives about things, that's all."

The sound of Dog barking interrupted her musings and she rose to continue unpacking boxes that had been shipped from her storage in St. Louis.

Baxter walked to the edge of Stone House's bluff and gazed across the sea. On September twenty-third, less than a week away, he would fly back to California. He bent to retrieve a stone and toss it into the ocean. He'd been miserable since his confrontation with Faith, and as much as he wanted to despise her and believe she was up to no good, he couldn't get his heart to agree with his head. After she'd moved out of the B & B, he'd hoped to find peace, but it never came. He picked up another stone to toss.

"Baxter," he heard his mother call out.

Surprised, he jerked around. "Mom, what are you doing here? Is something wrong?"

"Nothing's wrong. I just wanted to spend some time with my boy. You'll be gone soon and I won't see you until Christmas."

He joined his mother on the porch and she lifted a hand to his cheek. "Son, when are you going to come home to Somewhere? You know I'd give you complete authority over the B & B and someday it will be yours. What's keeping you away?"

Baxter covered her hand with his. "Honestly, I don't know, except that when I'm here, I remember all the dreams and goals I shared with Vanessa about the life and family we'd have in Somewhere. I guess being here reminds me of what could have been."

"But Baxter, that was years ago. It's time to relegate Vanessa to the past and start over." She turned her hand over and squeezed his. "In fact, I believed you

257

were back on track with Faith."

Baxter stepped away from his mother and turned to gaze at the setting sun. "Mom, I doubt she would even give me the time of day now. I've been terrible to her twice." His mother didn't reply and he continued watching rays of light cast sparkles across the ocean.

Finally, she said, "Baxter, I'm going to tell you something incredible, and because it's coming from me, I expect you to believe it." He heard her step closer. "Faith *did* talk to Owen."

Baxter whirled around. "How can you say that?"

"Because there's more to the story than you've heard." She inhaled and motioned toward two rocking chairs on the porch. "Let's sit while I tell you something impossible."

When his mother finished revealing the psychic's words and the entirety of Faith's encounter with a boy named Owen, including the part about Mr. Lucky's Grocery, Baxter was flabbergasted. He confronted his mother. "Mom, you don't really believe Owen is haunting our town, do you?" When she didn't answer he proclaimed, "Someone is playing a cruel joke and I intend to find out who it is!"

After his mother left, he spent a sleepless night at Stone House. If anything, her confession had eliminated any hostility toward Faith. At dawn he was dressed and following the trail back to the B & B where he nervously paced in his bedroom until he figured Faith was up. Before nine he was knocking on her door, and when she answered, dressed in jeans and an old T-shirt, his heart slammed his chest. She looked soft and vulnerable and he wanted to take her in his arms and beg her forgiveness. He wanted to explain that someone was carrying out a terrible hoax and he was going to discover the culprit, even if he had to postpone his return to California.

Instead of spilling his guts, however, he said, "The refurbishing of Stone

House is complete and I'd like to show it to you this afternoon. May I?" He watched her blink in confusion and hastily added, "I also want to apologize for my awful behavior. Something has come to light that we need to discuss. Can I pick you up around three?" Still looking confused, she nodded, and to make sure she didn't have time to change her mind, he rushed back to his car.

For the remainder of the day Baxter prepared for his afternoon with Faith. He called Seafood Heaven to place a takeout order of shrimp spaghetti and Italian bread, picked up the order, and then visited Genevieve's Flower Shop to buy a massive bouquet of pink roses and lilies. After that, he returned to Stone House to deliver their dinner, sweep the floors and porch, dust the mantle and furniture, and stock the hearth with logs. He then returned to the B & B to carry out his duties there.

While he was on the computer entering the previous day's expenses into the accounting program, his mother came into their sitting room and sat on the sofa. She watched him until he finally said, "I've asked Faith to Stone House this afternoon so I can apologize once again. If you want to say, 'I told you so,' you don't have to. I freely admit that I'm a jackass."

"So you believe us about Owen?"

"I believe that someone is playing an appalling joke."

His mother sighed. "Baxter, I hope you don't blow it again. Faith is a wonderful woman who is just now recovering from some terrible ordeal and—"

He interjected softly, "I know that, Mother, and I promise I won't hurt her again. If she wants to believe she's talking to a ghost, I'll not discredit her."

Gabby stood to leave. "I think this has been the strangest summer of my life."

"Yeah," Baxter murmured in agreement.

32: Sorry

At precisely three o'clock Baxter pulled to the front of Faith's house. When she opened the door at his knock, once again he was overwhelmed with both desire and compassion. He wanted to hold her, kiss her, and offer comfort for the sorrow she had suffered. Instead, he handed her the bouquet of roses and lilies and said, "Especially for you."

She appeared flustered. "Oh, my goodness! They're beautiful! Thank you! Please come in. I've been unpacking boxes from my storage unit in St. Louis that my sister was kind enough to ship. Have a seat while I put these flowers in water."

The house didn't have a foyer so he entered directly into the living room. He was impressed by its simple beauty and the stunning view beyond the glass slider. A circular area rug woven to depict sail boats with masts of many colors on a deep blue ocean covered the center of the hardwood floor. A tan sofa facing the view rested on the rug, and aqua chairs complemented either side of it. Pillows a shade lighter than the blue in the carpet were placed on the sofa and chairs. And other than two paintings showing different perspectives of beachgoers, there were no other pictures. Baxter walked to the slider to enjoy the view.

Faith returned after a few minutes with the flowers in a vase and set it on her fireplace mantle. "I found the living room ensemble at Chip's Furniture on Third Street and I've ordered a coffee and end tables from him."

Baxter tried to swallow the lump in his throat. When he considered his behavior toward this soft-spoken, beautiful woman who had suffered so much, he felt appalled. As far as he was concerned, she could believe she was talking to a dead boy and it wouldn't change the love he felt for her. "Your home is beautiful, Faith." He wanted to add, *And I've fallen in love with you,* but said instead, "May I walk outside?"

"Oh, yes! I wanted an ocean view and Doris and Dave delivered magnificently."

He opened the slider and stepped onto the patio. Faith followed and motioned to the outdoor furniture and they sat and gazed at the scene below—aqua ocean, sunbathers, colorful beach umbrellas, a few cars driving along Ocean Boulevard, and pedestrians walking the portion of Main Street visible from the house.

Baxter was about to break the silence when the back door to the house behind Faith's burst open and Darren and Dirk rushed outside. He glanced at Faith and she seemed to read his mind. She smiled slightly. "At first I talked myself out of buying this home because the boys reminded me so much of my own son, but gradually, since coming to Somewhere, something in me shifted, and in a moment of clarity I knew this was the home I was supposed to live in. It's still difficult at times hearing the boys play, but it's getting better." She bit her bottom lip and then confided, "And I have you to thank for that. Opening up to you and sharing my pain made me realize I *could* begin a new life."

Baxter felt his heart expand and reached to hold Faith's hand. "I'm so happy to hear that." He saw her eyes well with tears and quickly said, "Are you ready to see Stone House restored?"

She regained her composure. "I sure am."

As they walked to his car he said, "I ordered dinner from Seafood Heaven and it's waiting for us at Stone House. I know how much you like shrimp, so I ordered shrimp spaghetti." He grinned mischievously. "We can try heating it on the stove that's also been restored." He chuckled. "Or the microwave."

Faith laughed. "Have you tried out the stove yet?"

He winced. "Maybe we'll use the microwave tonight and experiment with the stove another time."

Baxter drove to the B & B and parked

in his reserved space. He said, "My mother is at her church preparing for a crafts fair and Jennie and James are at Costco in Brookings, so let's just head to Stone House."

"Sounds like a plan. But who's overseeing the B & B?"

"We're down to four guests and they all decided to drive to Gold Beach for the evening. Mabel said she still had some chores to finish so she offered to stay until my mother returned."

They exited the car and he punched his fob to lock it. Then he held Faith's elbow as he guided her to the sidewalk and crosswalk. Within minutes they had crossed the B & B's private beach and entered the coolness beneath the evergreens. Their stroll along the trail was melodic with birdsong, and sunlight filtering through the trees created crisscross patterns on the ground. Tangy sea air tickled their noses. Faith didn't say much and neither did he. Disturbing the sights and sounds of nature seemed irreverent.

When they arrived at Stone House, Faith walked to the edge of the bluff and turned around. With an expansive motion encompassing the house she exclaimed, "Your home is magnificent! I think your ancestors would be very proud of you."

Baxter had remained on the porch and now leaned against one of the new log posts. He watched the play of light on Faith's auburn hair and in a spontaneous gesture, opened his arms. For a moment she appeared puzzled by his action, but then understanding beamed across her countenance and she ran into his arms. He whispered in her ear, "I'm so sorry, Faith. Forgive me." And then he was kissing her.

Faith refused to analyze her actions because, for the first time in three years, she felt intact. She felt protected from the sorrow that had plagued her since the death of her family. She felt that once again she could live a happy life. But just as important, she knew she could give her heart to Baxter. Dinner was forgotten as he whispered words of love and then acted on those words by carrying her to the bedroom. Later he left the bed to light an oil lantern, but quickly returned to pull her back into his embrace. "I guess we'll have to spend the night at Stone House since it's too late to walk back."

Faith could feel him smile against her neck and she moved her mouth to whisper in his ear, "What do you think we should do until then?"

"I think we should perfect what we just did. You know the old adage—practice makes perfect."

"I thought it *was* perfect."

"Oh, baby, I love the way you talk. It was definitely a ten, but I think we should go for eleven and then twelve, and then–"

Faith placed her lips on his. "How about we don't set a limit?"

Baxter made a growling sound. "I also love the way you think."

Later, Faith woke with her head resting

on Baxter's shoulder and sighed with contentment. Her stomach growled and she decided to wake him and suggest they eat. She was about to say his name when she heard a voice.

"Rex! Rex!"

She inhaled sharply and found herself silently praying. *Please, God, no! I don't want to ruin my reunion with Baxter!*

"Rex!" The child's voice was louder than before and she jumped upright. Her movement woke Baxter and he said groggily, "What is it, baby?"

When she didn't respond he sounded more awake when he said, "Is something wrong?"

When she still didn't respond he sat up. "Faith, what is it?"

In a frightened voice she rasped, "I heard Owen again. I heard him calling for Rex."

Instantly, he encircled her with his arms, pulling her into the protection of his body. She knew he was waiting to hear the voice as she shivered against him.

269

There was only silence.

"Rex!"

Baxter exclaimed, "What the–"

"Rex! Come here boy!" There was a dog's bark in response.

Faith pushed away from Baxter. "You hear them?"

He jumped out of bed, pulled on his pants that were slung over a chair, and grabbed the lantern. "I sure as hell do and I'm going to get to the bottom of this nonsense. Stay here, Faith."

33: Truth

Before opening the door to the cabin, Baxter dimmed the lantern and shifted the curtain in the window next to the door to peer outside. He couldn't see anything because of the reflection, but heard a dog bark again, which electrified the hair on his arms. Then he got really angry, grabbed the lantern, and stormed out of the house, shouting, "Hey, you! I don't know what you're trying to accomplish by pretending to be a boy whose been dead for two decades, but I'm about to find out!"

"Hi, Bax," said a child's voice not far away. Baxter jumped and jerked in the direction of the voice. On the southern edge of the porch about twelve feet away, in the muted light cast by the lantern, stood Baxter's childhood friend, or at least someone who looked exactly like him, and a big red collie. The child knelt, picked up a Frisbee, and tossed it into the darkness of the yard. The dog yipped and ran after it.

Baxter quelled a strangled cry and demanded, "Who are you?"

The child replied, "I've waited a long time for you to hear me."

Baxter again vocalized his demand. "Who are you and who put you up to this?"

The child lowered himself Indian style onto the porch and placed his elbows on his knees and his chin in his palms. "Remember when we used to pretend to be Indians and camp out in the teepee your dad bought?"

Baxter took a step closer and then glanced across the yard calling out, "If anyone's hiding out there, you better step forward and tell me why you've put this kid up to this."

The only answer was the bark of the dog.

Baxter returned his gaze to the boy and took another step closer. The child was the exact image of Owen. "Explain yourself."

The boy heaved a heartfelt sigh. "What I've been trying to tell you since the accident is that I want my sister to know my death wasn't her fault. Tell Vee she isn't to blame."

Baxter decided to play along with the game. "Why don't you just tell her yourself?"

"Because things don't work like that. It would certainly make everything easier, but there's a purpose to the universe that cannot be changed. I guess you could say God wants to do things a certain way 'cause it's important. That's all I really know. Maybe I'll know the answer to your question when I walk into the light. But I won't go there until you believe me."

Baxter took another step closer and continued the game. "So why haven't I heard from you before now?"

"Because you needed Faith."

"I needed faith to believe or Faith the woman?"

The boy grinned. "Both."

Baxter glanced into the yard looking

for an accomplice, but saw no one. "Why would I need Faith the woman to allow me to see you?"

The child shrugged. "Beats me. When she saw Rex on the beach I was shocked. I'm always on the beach hoping someone will see us, like that other lady who stayed at the B & B. She knew we were there, but ignored us. I kept bugging her until she listened. She was nice and not after money like those phony psychics, but you were mean to her. After she left, I figured I'd always be in Somewhere, but then Faith saw me and I got hopeful again. And now here we are talking. It's a miracle."

Changing his tactic, Baxter said, "Why should I tell your sister your death wasn't her fault. No one ever blamed her."

"No, but she blamed herself. Still does. You see, she got mad at me and threw the Frisbee into the ocean. Rex went in after it and I followed him into the waves. She thinks I drowned because of that, but she's wrong. Rex got the Frisbee and we both got out of the water. Later, we followed the path to Stone House and I climbed down the rocks to the beach. My parents always warned me not to go there, but I disobeyed them this one time, and, well, paid the price. I tossed the Frisbee into the water and Rex got caught in an undertow. And when I tried to save him..." The boy locked his gaze with Baxter's. "...we both drowned."

Baxter's heart hammered at the likeness of this child to Owen. He crouched to the boy's level. "You expect me to believe that?"

"Of course. And when you tell my sister what I've told you, you'll both know it's really me."

They were interrupted when Rex bounded onto the porch with the Frisbee in his mouth. A sound from the doorway distracted Baxter and he turned to see Faith staring at them in disbelief. He stood to block her view of the boy because he didn't want her more upset than she already was, but when he

275

turned back around to grab the child by the scruff of his neck and haul him inside the cabin…

He was gone!

From beyond the shadows the child called out, "Tell Vee I'm sorry for reading her diary. And just so you know it's me, thanks for never telling anyone I egged Mr. Swift's car or that you were the one who wrote the love note to Annie for me."

34: Lighthouse

Lifting her paintbrush to the fourth and last painting Michael Wainwright had commissioned, Vicky signed her signature as Vee and stepped back. The scene was beautiful, even if she said so herself. In fact, she was extremely pleased with the way all the acrylic renditions of everyday life in Somewhere, both now and in the past, had turned out. This painting, however, was different because it was an ocean sunset, as requested by Michael. The colors were primarily orange and red, with splashes of yellow, and she'd actually painted the scene from atop Hope Hill. When she'd first started the project, she'd driven to the lookout and set up her easel with the intent of sketching the panorama and finishing it at home, however, the beauty had been such that she'd returned for a week and spent only today finishing it in her sitting room.

She gazed around the room at the rest

of the commissioned artwork leaning against the walls and sighed. Again, she was reminded of how much she loved to paint. She started cleaning her brushes, but was interrupted when she heard the doorbell ring. Since Faith often stopped by on Sunday afternoons, she assumed it was probably her. Wiping her hands on her apron, she hurried from her third floor suite and rushed downstairs. She was excited for Faith to see her finished sunset.

She reached the front door and peered through the peephole. It wasn't Faith. It was Michael Wainwright!

Smoothing a hand over her hair and sighing because she looked like hell, she cracked the door and then realized how rude that was. Opening the door wide, she said, "Hello, Mr. Wainwright."

He cocked his head to one side and grinned. "Michael, please."

His grin was so engaging that she returned it with a wide one of her own. "Michael, please come in." He surprised her when he said, "I was headed out for a drive along the coastline and wondered if you'd join me."

Vicky hadn't been asked to go anywhere with a man in years. "Ah, ah, how long would we be gone?"

"However long you want."

She felt herself blushing. "Um, that sounds nice."

His grin widened. "I was hoping you could point out some of the attractions outside of Somewhere. I hear there's a lighthouse about twenty miles away."

"Yes. It's lovely. I'd love to go there." She hesitated and said shyly, "I just finished the last painting."

Michael looked ecstatic. "May I see them?"

"Of course. But you'll have to follow me to the third floor." As she led the way upstairs she marveled at her trust in this man. Normally, she would have shied away from bringing a man upstairs, but in her heart she knew Michael was a good person. She opened the door to her sitting room and stepped inside. He followed and she motioned toward the easel. Biting her lip in nervousness she waited for his response. When he exclaimed, "I knew you had an exceptional talent when I first saw your paintings!" her heart sang. He stepped closer. "I absolutely love it!" He moved his gaze to the other acrylics, stepping in front of each one in turn. When he reached the last one he said, "Every painting is pure genius."

Vicky was so pleased by his admiration that she placed a hand over her heart and said breathlessly, "Thank you for your kind words."

Michael turned to face her. "Have you ever had an art exhibition exclusively for your paintings?"

She felt flustered. "No. I've never considered myself that good."

"Well you should. Why don't you think about it? I know several influential people in the art world."

Mortified, she replied, "Oh, I don't think

so. The first criticism would send me into tears."

Michael's expression softened. "And anyone who criticized would come into contact with my wrath." For a long moment he studied her face and then said cheerily, "There's no pressure. If you change your mind, just let me know and I'll get the ball rolling. Now, how long do you need to get ready? Should I wait downstairs or come back later?"

"It'll take me about twenty minutes. You can wait in the parlor if you like."

After Michael headed downstairs, Vicky entered her bathroom and gasped when she saw herself in the mirror. She had orange and red paint streaks on both cheeks.

At Cape Blanco in Cape Blanco State Park, Michael watched Vicky while listening to her history lesson. Her unassuming manner and shy smile wasn't something he was accustomed to. In his world of high finance, real estate deals, and schmoozing, she was a refreshing change.

Scanning a brochure she read, "The lighthouse was built in 1870 to warn mariners away from the reefs extending from the cape, and it stands on the farthest westerly point of the Oregon Coast, jutting one-and-a-half miles into the Pacific Ocean. The white cliffs are 200 feet high and were named by Spanish explorers."

Michael enjoyed listening to Vicky's condensed version of the history of the lighthouse, not only because it was so interesting, but because she enjoyed telling him. Her eyes came alive when she shared historical facts, which was something he'd noticed at the museum.

She said, "And the lighthouse is still in operation."

They left the interior of the structure and walked to the cliff's edge. Gazing across the sparkling ocean he said, "Vicky, have you ever painted a lighthouse?"

"No. Although I've considered doing so."

He waved a hand outwardly encompassing the blue expanse. "Can you imagine a ship lost at sea in the blackest of nights and a desperate crew suddenly coming upon this beacon of hope?" He felt Vicky's gaze and turned toward her.

Rather than answer his question she said, "Why is the ship lost? Was it a storm? Bad navigation?"

He sensed something deep in her question and smiled slightly. "How about both? First a storm took them off course and then in trying to correct their direction, they made things worse."

She glanced back out to sea and mused, "So even though they made bad decisions trying to get back on course, they were still saved."

"Precisely."

After a moment she said, "It would be a wonderful painting."

35: Fault

Reclining on her sofa, Vicky rehashed her day with Michael. He was a wonderful man and their visit to the lighthouse was something she would cherish.

Because of the scene evoked by Michael's words, she had privately decided to paint a lighthouse. The painting, however, would be more than just a ship and a lighthouse. Its very essence would be navigating the reefs of life to find haven in the midst of sorrow. Already she was planning to return to the site so she could paint under the presence of the lighthouse.

A tear trickled down her cheek because she knew the painting was for her. It was her way of navigating back into the stream of life. She would begin anew by using her paintbrush to stroke away the guilt that had consumed her since her brother's death. Another tear trickled and she whispered, "I'm so sorry, Owen."

Her cell phone rang and she gulped back tears. Taking a few seconds to compose herself, she finally answered the ringtone she recognized as being from Faith. "Hi, Faith."

"Hi, hon. I was wondering if you were free. Baxter and I would like to stop by."

"I'd love for you to come over. What time? I'll make some fresh tea and set out the cookies."

"Is two hours too soon?"

"Not at all. I'll see you then." Vicky hung up and smiled. It sounded like Baxter and Faith had resolved their differences and were back together.

Two hours later she opened the museum door and welcomed her friends, and although they smiled, she intuited that something was amiss. Had they not reconnected? If so, why were they together? They followed her upstairs to her sitting room where she had set out a tray of cookies and a pitcher of tea. "Have a seat while I grab some ice." She walked to her kitchen nook and opened the fridge.

Neither Baxter nor Faith said anything and Vicky was starting to feel apprehensive. Something was definitely wrong and somehow she was involved. She set a bowl of ice on the coffee table. "Why don't you go ahead and grab some cookies while I pour our tea?"

She was about to put ice in one of the glasses, when Baxter said, "Let's talk first."

Now she was feeling really anxious and expressed her concern. "Okay, something's going on. Both of you act like you're at a funeral." She stared into Baxter's eyes.

Baxter swiped a hand across his jaw, glanced at Faith, and finally said, "I don't even know how to begin."

Vicky frowned and looked at Faith. "Do you know what this is about?"

She nodded.

"Then why don't *you* begin?"

Faith pressed a finger against her left temple as if she had a headache.

286

Vicky leaned forward. "What the hell is going on?"

Faith's lips trembled when she said, "Yesterday, Baxter and I saw your brother Owen, and Baxter talked to him."

For a moment Vicky couldn't respond, but then she reared backward and shouted the obvious, "He's dead!"

Baxter joined the conversation. "I don't understand how it's possible, but Faith is telling the truth. We both saw him and Rex yesterday, and I talked to him."

Faith interjected, "He's been trying to get a message to you."

Jumping to her feet, Vicky stared at her friends. "Baxter, Faith, why are you doing this? You know how much his death devastated me and destroyed my family. Why would you want to hurt me like this?"

Baxter dropped a bombshell. "He told us to tell you his death wasn't your fault. You weren't the last person to throw the Frisbee into the water—he was."

Vicky had been about to ask Baxter

and Faith to leave when his words shocked her into collapsing back onto the sofa. She stared dumbfounded at her friends.

Twisting her hands in her lap, Faith said, "Let me start at the beginning and walk you through the events leading up to yesterday."

Over the next several minutes, Vicky learned about Faith's two personal encounters with Owen and Rex and the times she'd seen him from afar or heard him calling for his dog, and finally Baxter's encounter the day before that she had witnessed. Vicky also learned of Gabby's conversation with a psychic three years earlier. By the time Faith and Baxter were finished, Vicky felt drained and exhausted.

Baxter completed the story by saying, "One of the last things Owen said was, 'Tell Vee I'm sorry for reading her diary.'"

Vicky gasped and buried her face in her hands. It was time to confess what had happened during her last encounter with her brother. In faltering words she said, "We were at the beach and I...I was angry at him for reading my diary. It was late afternoon and no one was around because the season was over." She hesitated long enough to catch her breath. "I picked up the Frisbee and tossed it as far out into the waves as I could and...and Owen yelled at me, calling me Vee, which I hated, and said I was being mean. I made a face at him as Rex was running into the waves." She swiped her tears and sobbed, "Then Owen ran after Rex and that was the last time I saw them, because I didn't wait for them to get out of the water."

Faith left her chair and came to sit beside Vicky. She placed her arm around her. Vicky allowed herself the comfort and said against Faith's shoulder, "I've always believed that my brother's drowning, and then my family falling apart, was because of me."

Faith smoothed Vicky's hair. "Honey, I don't understand what's happened, but

Owen wants you to know his death wasn't your fault. It wasn't anyone's fault. It was an accident. It–" Suddenly Faith stopped speaking and began crying. Her crying turned into a wail and Vicky leaned forward grasping her friend by the shoulders. "Faith, what's wrong?"

With lightening speed, Baxter moved to the couch and sat on the other side of Faith. "Honey, talk to me!"

While Faith continued weeping, both Baxter and Vicky tried to ascertain what was wrong. On a huge shudder Faith said, "I've been doing the same thing. I've blamed myself for my husband's and child's deaths. I never told anyone that the night of the crash my husband wasn't feeling well, so I offered to drive, but he insisted it wasn't necessary." She sobbed, "I shouldn't have listened to him. Hammond sometimes had migraines that blurred his vision, and I know that's what happened. The report said he veered into oncoming traffic and then overcorrected, sending the car into a tree..." Her voice trailed. "But I was watching a documentary on television that I didn't want to miss." She cried out, "I should have been driving the car! My selfishness killed them!"

Baxter returned from the bathroom with a Kleenex box and sat between Vicky and Faith. He placed an arm around each of them, and for a long time no one said anything as they realized their years of turmoil had finally come to an end. Objectively, he could now see his own shortcomings that had played a role in his divorce. He knew that much of the antagonism he'd directed toward his ex-wife was really frustration over his own inadequacies and immaturity.

Aloud he said, "In all of our tragedies there was the probability they could have been averted if different choices were made, and had we known the future, we *would* have chosen differently. But the bottom line is that Owen returned to teach us something. He taught us that

291

unforeseen results often happen because decisions are made in anger as with Vicky, or ignorance as with Faith, or willful ignorance as with me. But in each case none of us could foresee the dreadful outcomes, and if we could change our responses, we would in a heartbeat. Owen's message is that it's time to move on; it's time to release the past because living with guilt will not change anything. It will only destroy three more lives." He pulled Faith and Vicky closer. "The question we have to ask ourselves now is how do we want to shape our futures?"

36: Disclosure

Vicky woke feeling great. A week after Baxter and Faith's amazing revelation, she no longer felt weighted by her brother's death. By some miracle he had remained behind to send her a message, and that message had not only been for her, but for Baxter and Faith, as well. It was time to stop existing and start living. She sighed and mused over the paradox that her dead brother had renewed her life. Because that revelation was too overwhelming to ponder at the moment, she decided to shower and dress and do something she'd been thinking about for a while.

She took her time dressing and then sat leisurely at the tiny table in her sitting room drinking coffee. Finally, she opened her laptop and typed two words into a Google search: Michael Wainwright. Her internet connection was slow and she held her breath while the response chugged out.

From her first meeting with Michael she'd felt attracted to him, and after their visit to the lighthouse, she'd gotten the notion that he was also feeling something for her. Maybe it was just friendship, but she'd welcome that. Perhaps they could become friends like she was with Baxter. It was time to expand her horizons. Michael had given the impression that he was a man of experience, so he was the perfect candidate for asking questions about the world beyond Somewhere. She might even consider taking him up on his suggestion that she have a showing of her artwork.

The landing page of her search flashed onscreen and she read the bio in the sidebar.

The CEO and major stockholder of Wainwright Resorts, Inc. is Michael Wainwright, III.

She furrowed her brow and clicked on the link. By the time she'd finished

294

reading she was livid, not only with Michael, but with herself for being so gullible. The part that hurt, however, was his passion for filling his resorts with the works of local artists, and since many artists had been discovered in that way, they clamored to be included among his collections. He'd told her, "I'm well connected to connoisseurs in the art world; yours will be seen by them."

Vicky felt ill. She had surmised that her paintings would be displayed in his home. But now that she knew his identity, there was only one conclusion. *He wants to build a resort in Somewhere and hang my paintings there!*

Grabbing her cell phone she tapped her contacts icon and located his name. He answered on the second ring. "Hello, Vicky. What a pleasant surprise. Have you decided to accept my offer of an art show?"

"Are you building a resort in Somewhere?"

He hesitated. "A resort hasn't been

approved, but I'm hopeful it will be."

"And you're going to display my paintings there?"

Another pause. "Yes. They're wonderful."

"I want them back and I'll return every penny you paid me."

"I can't return them."

"Can't or won't?"

"Won't."

Vicky could hear tears in her voice when she said, "We don't want a resort in Somewhere and I adamantly don't want my paintings displayed there. It would appear as if I'd colluded with the enemy to destroy our town."

"You're being melodramatic. And I'm not going to destroy your town. I'm going to enhance it. I want to become part of it. That's why I purchased a home there."

Vicky swallowed her tears, inhaled deeply, and resolutely said, "Then I'll fight you every step of the way." Before he could respond, she disconnected.

Epilogue

Faith sat on her towel on the beach. Fall was well underway so the mornings were cool, but there was still a space of time each afternoon that was warm enough for beach lazing. She sighed with contentment. She was almost finished writing the romance that she'd titled *Dax and the Duchess,* and was thinking about asking Gabby to read it. Perhaps she'd even garner the courage to let Baxter read it, since he was her inspiration.

Baxter had returned to California, but only to prepare for a permanent move to Somewhere. Faith smiled when she remembered their parting only a week earlier. He'd held her so tenderly and spoken such beautiful words that she'd cried. Upon seeing her tears, he'd been mortified and apologized for whatever he'd said. Lovingly, she had smiled and cupped his cheeks. "I'm crying because I'm so happy."

At her confession, he'd pulled her

close again and whispered, "I love you, Faith, and I'm never letting you go. You've given me back my dreams, my hopes, my life."

Returning her thoughts to the present, Faith gazed southward along the shoreline. Tourist season was over so only a handful of beachgoers remained. She moved her gaze past a mother and child playing in the waves...and blinked. Then she gasped! A large red dog leaped upward to catch a Frisbee. She searched for whoever had thrown the toy and not far away was a boy wearing a blue ball cap. She couldn't breathe. And then, adding to her shock, the boy was joined by another boy. The dog reached the children and dropped the Frisbee in front of the second child. Immobilized, she watched him pick up the Frisbee and toss it. The dog barked and ran after it. Faith couldn't remove her eyes from the child until she saw a man walking toward him. She recognized his gait, and although she wanted to run toward the children and the man, she knew she couldn't.

The dog returned with the Frisbee and dropped it in front of the man. He squatted to retrieve it, but glanced up, staring directly at her. She wasn't close enough to perceive his facial features, but she knew beyond a doubt that he was smiling. Tears clouded her vision as she moved her gaze to the children, who were also watching her. She knew they were smiling, too. The three of them raised their hands and waved, and then the man stood and tossed the Frisbee high in the air before placing an arm around each boy as they turned to walk down the beach.

Faith watched the trio recede into the distance to be joined again by the dog, and she knew that if she glanced away, they would be gone. Could she let them go?

She moved her gaze to the water and then back to the beach. They were gone.

Author's Note

For a while it was touch and go with Baxter Hope and Faith Bennison, but the fact that they were able to overcome past sorrows and find happiness once again, did my heart good. No doubt their relationship will face obstacles, as does every relationship, but their foundation of love will sustain them. I'm sure of it.

As for Gabby Hope's dilemma with Leo Constanzo, I'm not sure how that will turn out. She's a strong woman with a sense of right and wrong that may be somewhat off course. Will Leo continue his pursuit of the woman he loves, or come to believe his quest is a lost cause?

And now that Victoria Patterson is no longer plagued by guilt over her brother's death, I was hoping she and Michael Wainwright might discover romance. However, with his desire to build a resort in Somewhere, and Vicky discovering his plan to display her paintings at the resort, that may not be possible. She's livid and intends to do everything she can to block approval for the resort.

Thank goodness this is the first book in the *Finding SOMEWHERE Series* because it gives me plenty of time to resolve these issues, create more issues, and introduce new characters with each book.

I love hearing from readers, so don't be shy.

www.vernaclay.com
vernaclay@vernaclay.com

Join Mailing List:
http://www.vernaclay.com/mailing-list.html

Novels and Novellas by Verna Clay

CONTEMPORARY ROMANCE

<u>Western</u>

Romance on the Ranch Series
Dream Kisses
Honey Kisses
Baby Kisses
Candy Kisses
Christmas Kisses
Rock Star Kisses
Forever Kisses
Forgotten Kisses
Angel Kisses
The Last Kiss

Oasis, Arizona Series
Stranded in Oasis
Branded in Oasis
Crashed in Oasis

<u>Paranormal</u>

Finding SOMEWHERE Series
SOMEWHERE *by the Sea*
SOMEWHERE *to Spend Christmas*

SOMEWHERE *for a Hero to Hide*
SOMEWHERE *to Begin Again (coming soon)*

HISTORICAL ROMANCE

Unconventional Series
Abby: Mail Order Bride
Broken Angel
Ryder's Salvation
Joy's Return
2014 Gold Medal Winner Readers' Favorite
Int'l Book Contest/Historical Romance

Finding Home Series
Cry of the West: Hallie
Rescue on the Rio: Lilah
Missouri Challenge: Daisy

Red Rocks Trilogy: Past Present Future
Healing Woman of the Red Rocks (Past)
Song of the Red Rocks (Present)
Spirit Tree of the Red Rocks (Future)

FANTASY ROMANCE

Shapeling Trilogy
Roth: Protector (Book 1)
Fawn: Master (Book 2)
Davide: Prince (Book 3)

303

Jazmine

YOUNG ADULT ROMANCE
(Verna Clay writing as Colleen Clay)

Fragile Hearts

AUDIO BOOKS

Abby: Mail Order Bride
Broken Angel
Cry of the West: Hallie
Dream Kisses

LARGE PRINT PAPERBACK

SOMEWHERE *by the Sea*
SOMEWHERE *to Spend Christmas*
SOMEWHERE *for a Hero to Hide*
SOMEWHERE *to Begin Again*
(coming soon)

Printed in Great Britain
by Amazon

53025906R00179